TRUCKDOGS

In a far-off desert world remarkably similar to outback Australia, evolution has taken an unexpected turn. The dominant life form is a creature covered in fur but with living steel panels beneath. It gnaws on bones and sniffs lampposts but fills up on oil, brake fluid and petrol. And it's wonderfully clever with its wheels and wing mirrors – able to do just about anything, in fact – which is lucky since it hasn't got any arms or legs.

It's an animal with an engine. Or is it a car with floppy ears and a wet nose?

This is the world of TruckDogs.

By the same author

My Grandma Lived in Gooligulch

Animalia

The Eleventh Hour

The Sign of the Seahorse

The Discovery of Dragons

The Worst Band in the Universe

The Waterhole

TRUCK DOGS

A NOVEL
IN FOUR
BITES

Graeme Base

VIKING

an imprint of

PENGUIN BOOKS

Viking

Published by the Penguin Group
Penguin Books Australia Ltd
250 Camberwell Road
Camberwell, Victoria 3124, Australia
Penguin Books Ltd
80 Strand, London WC2R 0RL, England
Penguin Putnam Inc.
375 Hudson Street, New York, New York 10014, USA
Penguin Books, a division of Pearson Canada
10 Alcorn Avenue, Toronto, Ontario, Canada M4V 3B2
Penguin Books (NZ) Ltd
Cnr Rosedale and Airborne Roads, Albany, Auckland, New Zealand
Penguin Books (South Africa) (Pty) Ltd
24 Sturdee Avenue, Rosebank, Johannesburg 2196, South Africa
Penguin Books India (P) Ltd
11, Community Centre, Panchsheel Park, New Delhi 110 017, India

First published by Penguin Books Australia Ltd 2003

1 3 5 7 9 10 8 6 4 2

Typeset in 13/19 pt Joanna by Post Pre-press Group, Brisbane, Queensland
Printed in Singapore by Imago Productions
Colour reproduction by Splitting Image, Clayton, Victoria

National Library of Australia
Cataloguing-in-Publication data:

Base, Graeme, 1958– .
Truckdogs.

ISBN 0 670 89333 1.

1. Vehicles – Juvenile fiction. 2. Australia – Juvenile fiction. I. Title.

A823.3

www.puffin.com.au

For William

CONTENTS

List of

ILLUSTRATED PLATES

PAW WORD

What is it with dogs and cars? Dogs love cars, love chasing after them, love travelling in them, love peeing on the wheels, love barking as they roar by. At least our dog Molly does. So it shouldn't have come as such a shock when I found a stack of dog-eared paper at the back of her kennel that turned out to be a first draft manuscript entitled *TruckDogs*.

As I pawed through the pages, brushing away dog hair and the occasional flea, it all fell into place – the furtive notes I had seen her making on long road trips, the twelve-month subscription to *Big Rig* magazine that I know wasn't mine, and the paw prints on the kids' computer keyboard. They say everyone has a novel in them and clearly our Molly was no exception.

But when she announced she wanted her book published I had my doubts and I told her so. She was barking up the wrong tree, I said. Publishing was a dog-eat-dog world, no bones about it. But she ignaw-ed me.

Finally, I relented and agreed to show the work to my

publisher. The reaction was as I had feared. 'TruckDogs?' they asked. 'What are they? Where did they come from? And how do they do all those things like pump petrol and throw spanners without the benefit of opposable thumbs?'

I confronted Molly but she had no answers. Perhaps if I was to draw some pictures it would help? she suggested. I told her it was out of the question. Then she did that thing dogs do with their big doleful eyes and long floppy ears and tail half-wagging in forlorn hope. And I rolled over.

So here it is – Molly's first novel. With pictures. Every dog has its day.

GB 2003

BITE ONE

'This is such a bad idea,' said Bullworth, peering out from the long, dry grass that swept down from the hill towards the dam. He flicked an ear nervously and fidgeted with his rear drive wheels. 'We shouldn't be doing this.'

Bullworth was big as TruckDogs go, a bulldog/dozer with a huge mouth, chunky caterpillar tracks and a thick stumpy tail. Like all TruckDogs he was half vehicle, half dog. He ran on diesel, plus some oil for his hydraulics, but unlike his Mongrel Pack friends who scoffed dog food and gnawed on old bones, Bullworth was a vegetarian and ate cabbages by the tonne.

The other TruckDogs were silent, intent, crouched low in the grass. They were a motley collection of makes and breeds, young enough to still have their original tyres, old enough to be sporting lots of scratches and several impressive dents.

None of them had much fat on the bones, however. Without homes of their own they had to fend for themselves, sleeping under the stars, picking up meals where they could, getting by on the smell of an oily rag.

Beyond the fence at the bottom of the hill, a flock of TruckSheep grazed quietly on the lusher grass that grew near the water. It was a peaceful scene, the morning sun glowing on the fence posts that ran from the paddock up to Farmer Howell's farmhouse on the neighbouring hill.

'Relax,' said Prudence, seeing Bullworth's worried expression. 'We're only chasing them, not eating them.'

Prudence was a slender dachshund/fuel-tanker road train. Her shiny black bodywork was set off by purple fenders and underbelly and a pair of tall chrome exhaust stacks behind her long ears. She turned to Bullworth with a smile. 'Unless you *want* to eat them instead?'

'No!' he said, shocked. He looked again at the TruckSheep. 'But they're huge – and they've got horns. I don't wanna get hurt.'

Zoe, the other girl in the Mongrel Pack, a streetwise dalmatian/cement mixer with blue spots and purple eyeshadow, shook her head and shoved the gum she was chewing to the side of her grille. 'Aw, don't be such a sook, Bullworth. You're made of solid iron and you're worried about getting a couple of dents?'

'He's right, y'know,' offered Digger. 'Sheep-leaping can be dangerous – but only if you get caught.'

Digger was a labrador/back hoe, good-natured like all labs, sand-coloured, with a brown nose and a ready smile. He

4

winked at Bullworth, his long pink tongue lolling out. 'C'mon, mate, those TruckSheep are no match for you.' He scratched suddenly behind his ear with his rear excavator shovel. 'Flies are driving me nuts.'

'Flies?' said Prudence. 'What you've got there is *fleas*. When's the last time you had a car wash?'

Digger shrugged. 'I dunno. What month is it?'

'Zip it, you lot.' Hercules frowned at the other TruckDogs. He was the self-appointed leader of the Pack, a massive great dane/ore truck. 'Let's see if we can retain the element of surprise here, all right?'

'Sure, Herc,' said Zoe, revving coyly.

'Sure, Herc,' said Prudence and Digger, winking at each other.

Bullworth looked unhappy.

Hercules nodded. 'Okay. Everyone together. Ready . . . Set . . . Go!'

The TruckDogs burst from cover and raced down the hill towards the grazing TruckSheep, baying like wolves, horns blaring, engines roaring. The TruckSheep looked up at the noise and scowled, baring old, yellow teeth. These were no lambs – meek and easily frightened – but big, tough TruckSheep.

'Woo hoo!' yelled Digger as he dropped himself into overdrive and slewed round an outcrop of boulders.

'Yeehaa!' cried Prudence, leaping right over the outcrop, ears flapping in the wind as she carved a graceful arc through the air.

The TruckSheep baaa-ed angrily, turned towards the intruders, put their heads down and charged.

'Okay, split up!' yelled Hercules.

The TruckDogs fanned out, racing across the paddock in big sweeping curves, drawing the TruckSheep in different directions until there were sheep and dogs zooming everywhere.

A TruckSheep veered away from the main flock.

'That one's got your name on it, Digger!' called Prudence.

Digger dropped back a gear, dug in his wheels and made a sharp turn to bring himself alongside the galloping TruckSheep. He dodged this way and that as the beast tried to skewer him with its horns or trample him under-wheel, then, pulling away slightly, he slowed and gathered himself for a leap. But suddenly Hercules roared past him, springing over the TruckSheep with a huge bound and crashing to the ground on the other side. He just missed Bullworth, who was rumbling by in the other direction trying to get out of the way.

The TruckSheep bleated in surprise and took off.

'Hey, watch it. You nearly hit me,' said Bullworth.

'If I'd meant to hit you, you'd be on your roof,' replied Hercules.

'One to our great leader,' said Prudence.

'You are just so good at this, Herc,' said Zoe. Hercules looked pleased with himself.

Digger shrugged and looked around for another target.

The game continued. The young TruckDogs dodged and revved, swerved and leapt, chancing their luck with the angry TruckSheep, and adding several new scratches and dents to their bodywork.

Prudence raced along in a great curve, pursued by three furious TruckSheep. Suddenly she twisted and launched herself into the air, bounding across all three of them, one after the other, zigzag, like a big move on a draughts board.

'Three!' she yelled. 'Now who's looking good?'

'Nice one,' called Digger. 'But I've got seven.'

'Herc is up to ten,' said Zoe.

Bullworth shook his head as he watched the other Mongrels racing around the paddock. 'They're all nuts.'

On the far side of the dam, on a low rise, lay an old tanker hulk, rusting in the sun. From the top another TruckDog was watching the Mongrel Pack, his short tail wagging at high speed. He was a little Jack Russell/ute, brown and white, very excited, with a bright-red collar and a shiny name tag. His name was Sparky.

He bounced up and down on his springs, trying to get a better view. 'Oh, boy! Sheep-leaping. I love this!'

He jumped down from the tanker and squeezed through the fence wire, disappearing into the long grass as he sped around the edge of the dam towards the others.

Sparky knew the Mongrels were what his mum called 'problem kids' – always in trouble, a source of constant irritation to the good townsfolk of Hubcap – but he couldn't help liking them. It wasn't their fault they had no homes of their own. They were just regular kids. And they had the best fun doing cool things like sheep-leaping.

'Hey, guys! Hi! Can I play?' he yapped as he burst out of the tussocks and skidded to a stop, tail wagging faster than ever.

The TruckSheep had given up the chase for the time being and were standing together at the other side of the paddock, breathing heavily.

Prudence looked at Sparky and shrugged. 'Sure, why not?'

'Because he's too small,' said Hercules. 'Because he'll probably get killed. Because he's not part of the Pack.'

The wagging tail slowed.

'Come on, Herc,' said Digger. 'Worst that can happen is he gets totally written off. Or caught.'

'Hey, Sparky,' said Zoe. 'Does your mum know you're here?'

Sparky winced. 'She thinks I'm cleaning out my room.'

He was an obedient son, as a rule, but today he felt justified in skipping this chore – he'd cleaned his room just the other week. Well, back in February anyway. Besides, the day was too good to spend indoors.

'You're going to cop it,' said Prudence. 'Tell her we kidnapped you.'

'She'd believe it,' said Sparky. His mum was the Mayor of

Hubcap – and she didn't approve of him hanging around with the Mongrel Pack, even though he was only a year or so younger than they were.

'Hey, look,' said Digger, nodding towards the TruckSheep. They had gathered together by the fence in a rough line. 'Y'know, I reckon I could clear the lot of them in one go the way they are now.'

'Not if I get there first,' said Hercules. And he sped away, shoving Digger to one side.

'They're mine, you dirty sheep thief!' called Digger. He crunched into gear and roared after him.

'C'mon, Zoe,' laughed Prudence. 'We can't let the boys have all the glory!'

They tore off, leaving Sparky and Bullworth behind.

'Count me out,' said the big bulldozer.

The TruckDogs hurtled towards the TruckSheep. But all at once Hercules skidded to a stop.

'Hold on, I smell a ram.'

The others put on the brakes. Suddenly Sparky shot past, yelling excitedly. 'Come on, guys! What are you waiting for?'

He raced up to the TruckSheep, yapping like mad. The sheep looked at him balefully, then moved apart. Behind them stood a huge, snorting beast, solid muscle and steel, cruelly curved horns mounted above massive bony fenders: the TruckRam from hell.

Sparky gulped.

The huge TruckRam tore at the ground with his front

wheels. Sparky slammed his gearbox into reverse, spun around in a cloud of dust and bolted back across the paddock. The TruckRam set off after him.

'Not this way, you idiot!' cried Hercules.

'Go left!' yelled Prudence.

'Or right!' added Digger.

'Anywhere but here!' screamed Zoe.

The TruckDogs turned and fled, Bullworth with them. But Sparky quickly caught up, terrified, the huge TruckRam breathing down his exhaust pipe.

'Help!'

'Head for the dam!' yelled Digger.

They raced across the paddock, shock absorbers crashing and bouncing on the uneven ground, and launched themselves into the air. The TruckRam lunged at Sparky as he leapt, sending him spinning.

A moment later the still waters of the dam erupted in a series of huge splashes as the TruckDogs disappeared into the muddy depths.

The TruckRam skidded to a stop at the water's edge and snorted in satisfaction as the intruders floundered in the middle of the dam. Then he turned and motored back across the paddock with his nose in the air.

The TruckDogs reached the far side of the dam and hauled themselves out, coughing and spluttering. Bullworth sat sobbing in the shallows.

'I'm . . . all . . . wet. I'm going to die of rust.'

Zoe dragged herself up the bank, dripping and covered in weeds, muddy water sloshing out of her mixer.

'Look at me!' she screeched. 'I'm filthy!'

She splashed angrily, sending more mud flying into her own face, and burst into tears. The others scrambled up the slope and collapsed in a sodden heap. Prudence looked around.

'Where's Sparky?'

'Who cares?' sulked Zoe, turning on her wipers but only managing to smear mud all over her windscreen.

Digger reached down with his back hoe and felt around in the water. After a moment he scooped Sparky out and dumped him on the grass.

'Here he is.'

'Thanks,' said Sparky, gasping.

'No worries.'

But Hercules was not so easygoing. 'Should have left him there. Brainless dipstick.'

Sparky hung his head. The others shook themselves dry like dogs do. Zoe screeched as she got spattered with mud again.

'Hey, look on the bright side,' said Digger as they sat there, dripping.

'And what bright side would that be exactly?' inquired Prudence.

'We could've been caught by Windy Howell.'

Prudence laughed. 'Yeah, downwind. That old pick-up can backfire like no other TruckDog alive.'

At that very moment a bang rang out across the paddock like a gunshot. They looked at each other in dread.

On the hill beyond the TruckSheep paddock, an old red heeler/Ford pick-up emerged from his run-down farmhouse. The screen door slammed behind him. He revved his engine and let rip another deafening backfire. Flames and smoke billowed out of his exhaust pipe, as he looked across the fields towards the dam.

'It's that flea-bitten Mongrel Pack again,' growled Farmer Howell. 'I'll teach them to worry my sheep!'

He unleashed another flatulent masterpiece, setting fire to a stump by the outhouse and at the same time propelling himself down the hill towards the dam.

Prudence watched Farmer Howell career across the field towards them in a cloud of billowing oily smoke and shook her head.

'One of these days he's going to blow himself up.'

'I'm getting out of here!' cried Bullworth.

'Too right,' said Digger, and the others agreed. Angry TruckRams were one thing – Farmer Howell on the warpath was something else altogether.

They turned tail and fled.

TRUCK**DOGS**

Reg No. 45865 k9

NAME: SPARKY

BREED/MAKE: Jack Russell/Ute
COLOUR: Brown and white
IDENTIFYING MARKS: Bright-red collar, waggy tail
TEMPERAMENT: V. enthusiastic

FILE INFO:
11 years old. Son of Mayor Plugg. Lives with mother (76 Boneo Rd, Hubcap). Father deceased. Good kid but overly influenced by local street gang (Mongrel Pack).

SPECIFICATIONS:
Engine: 4-cylinder, 1600cc
Fuel Requirements: Unleaded petrol, standard dog food plus the occasional bone
Maintenance: 12-month oil change & flea treatment
Regular worming (monthly)

'The trouble with the youth of today is they have no respect,' said Edna Fleasome as she bustled out of Hubcap general store with a roof-rack loaded with groceries.

'No respect,' agreed her sister, Ida.

'They don't even have homes.'

'No homes.'

'They don't belong here.'

Ida nodded.

'And they're dirty,' Edna said with conviction.

'Dirty,' echoed Ida.

The two sisters motored out into the main street, a wide, dusty strip of red dirt flanked by a ragged line of weather-board and corrugated-iron buildings. Next door to the general store was the local bone depot. Across the road stood Scratchly's Fencing Supplies. Further up was the Country TruckDogs' Association building and a couple of houses with low verandahs shielding their windows from the desert sun. The only permanent-looking building in the street was the Town Hall that stood on the corner of Memorial Park. It had an entrance porch with two white pillars and a curved ramp leading to its double doors.

The only other notable features of the town were the park itself (a statue of Lord Hubcap stood in the middle behind a rope fence), a creaking windmill, and several rusty water tanks. At the far end of the main street stood Hubcap Garage. It was the only petrol station in town (two pumps: one standard, one diesel). A fuel shed stood to one side and a large mechanics workshop was set back to the right.

Beyond the petrol station the road stretched out to the distant horizon – the Great Outback Highway that led to Combustion City far to the south.

Edna and Ida drove past some young TruckPups playing in the road, laughing and rolling about in the dust. Edna shook her head.

'They should be in obedience school,' she tut-tutted.

'Obedience school,' agreed Ida.

At that moment the sound of thumping music was heard, growing louder. Edna looked up the street and scowled.

'Come, Ida. We don't need to listen to this.' They turned and drove off.

The Mongrel Pack rolled into town. A sign hanging over the roadway said 'Welcome to Hubcap' and beneath, in smaller letters, 'Hubcap is a Tidy Town. Please dispose of your droppings thoughtfully'. One by one the TruckDogs sprang up and hit the sign with a wing mirror as they passed underneath. The hinges squeaked in protest as the sign swung back and forth. Sparky, following the older TruckDogs at the end of the line, jumped up as well. He didn't quite reach it.

Zoe's radio was on full blast. The TruckDogs shimmied from side to side in time with the music, stirring up clouds of dust, as they came down the street. *Thump! Thump! Thump!*

Mr Scratchly, a rather deaf bitzer/hatchback, came out of the fencing-supplies store and scowled at the noise, fiddling with his hearing aid. 'Twurn that racket down!' he called.

'Eh, what's that?' shouted Hercules. 'Can't hear you.'

'Bah!' Mr Scratchly turned and went back inside. The Mongrels motored on.

Edna and Ida turned and watched from the roadside, tut-tutting as the Pack went by.

'Morning, Miss Fleasome, Miss Fleasome,' said Digger pleasantly, nodding at the two sisters.

Edna turned away primly. 'Insolent pup, talking to an adult that way. You can tell their parents never taught them manners. And all that ruckus,' she continued. 'Wasting fuel – goodness knows there's barely enough to go round as it is. I don't know what this town is coming to.'

Ida's echo was lost as the Mongrel Pack rolled by and continued on down the street. *Thump! Thump! Thump!*

The Pack passed the Town Hall and turned left into Memorial Park.

Sparky followed, but as he went past the Town Hall a matronly Irish setter/Land Rover Discovery called out from the top of the steps. She was wearing a blue sash with a large gold medallion of office. Mayor Plugg. Sparky's mum.

'Sparky. Here, boy.'

Sparky pretended not to hear.

'Sparky, I know you can hear me. I've just had a call from Farmer Howell . . .'

Sparky cringed.

Mrs Plugg looked across her desk at her son. He squirmed uncomfortably. A photo of him as a TruckPup stood to one side of her desk. On the other side was a photo of Mr and Mrs Plugg on their wedding day.

'Sparky, I've told you a hundred times about that Mongrel Pack,' said Mrs Plugg. 'I know they're, well, disadvantaged . . . but they'll only get you into trouble.'

'We were just having some fun,' protested Sparky. 'Having a bit of a run . . . and jump.'

Mayor Plugg looked squarely at her son. 'Farmer Howell says you were harassing his TruckSheep.'

'More like them harassing us.'

Mayor Plugg shook her head. 'What am I going to do with you?'

'That's the problem, Mum – there's nothing to do round here.'

'Well then, I'll find you something to do,' she said briskly. 'Go over to the petrol station and collect those drums of anti-rust I ordered. That new mechanic, Rex Whatever-his-name-is, should know about it. Then you can tidy your room – I assume you haven't done it yet? It looks like a DesertDog has been holed up in it. And clean out the food bowls from breakfast. Go on now. I've a mountain of work to get through.'

Mayor Plugg busied herself at her desk. Sparky rolled his eyes.

'Don't roll your eyes at me,' said Mrs Plugg without looking up.

How do mothers do that? wondered Sparky as he headed back into the street. He dragged his wheels as he went. Mrs Plugg glanced at the photo of her and Mr Plugg.

'A pup needs a father,' she sighed.

The sun was beating down. Sparky crossed to the shady side of the street. He paused to sniff a couple of verandah posts on the way. The posts heading in the other direction were more interesting and he began to wander back up the street.

Soon he had made his way up to the general store. A little TruckBug buzzed past his ear. Sparky snapped at it, springing up and bumping into a water trough by the verandah. The trough slipped off its footings onto the ground and tipped over, sending water sloshing across the verandah and up against the walls.

'Oops.'

The storekeeper was out in a flash. He was a bad-tempered corgi/delivery van with a squint in one eye.

'Look at this!' snapped Mr Barker, nostrils flaring indignantly. 'Don't you know there's a drought?'

'Sorry,' said Sparky. 'It was an accident.' He pushed the trough back upright with his bumper bar. The remains of the water splashed out over Mr Barker's wheels.

'Watch it!' cried the storekeeper, jumping back. 'Kids. Should be banned.' He turned, shaking his rear wheels dry, and disappeared irritably back into the shop.

A middle-aged basset hound/mobile crane and his wife, a spaniel/tray truck with a handy scissor-lift attachment, chugged up the street. They looked at hapless Sparky and shook their heads good-naturedly.

'The Plugg boy,' observed Mr Dogsbody.

Mrs Dogsbody nodded and sighed. 'Poor Mayor Plugg. It can't be easy.'

Sparky hurried now down to the petrol station and across to the workshop. The workshop was a big weatherboard building with wide barn doors and a high window above. A faded banner read 'Smash Repairs – All Models, Makes and Breeds. Mechanic on duty.' An 'Open' sign hung on a nail underneath.

The big doors were open wide. Just inside, an old and weatherworn red setter/tractor was working on the engine of a border collie/combine harvester. The tractor was a scruffy sort – patches of rust showing through faded red paintwork, mismatched wheels with worn tyres, a bent funnel sticking up above his greying snout. As Sparky approached he looked up and wiped his front wheels on an oily rag.

'Hiya, Rex!' said Sparky. 'What are you doing? I've been hanging out with the Mongrel Pack. Boy, we had fun! We were sheep-leaping, and we got chased by this huge ram right into the dam, and Farmer Howell nearly caught us, but we got out of there really fast, I can tell you! And then Mum found out – that's the not-so-good bit – but she was pretty cool about it, and she told me to come over here and get some, er, axle grease or something that she's ordered so . . .' he stopped for a breath. 'So I've come over to get it.' He noticed the combine harvester. 'So what're you doing? Fixing someone?'

Rex was already back working on the engine, delicately adjusting the fanbelt with his worn old front tyres. 'Yup.'

'Got him working yet?'

'Nup.'

Sparky looked with interest at the engine.

'Think you can?'

'Yup.'

'Can I help?'

Rex turned and regarded Sparky for a moment. He crossed to the cluttered workshop wall where some cans were stacked in long rows, nudged three drums of anti-rust off the shelf with his snout and into Sparky's tray. He looked at the little ute from under his bushy eyebrows, waiting for him to go, but Sparky just smiled and wagged his tail.

Rex sighed and turned back to the harvester. 'You can pass me that spanner.'

Rex had only been in Hubcap a week or two. He had turned up out of nowhere, a drifter, it seemed, who moved from town to town, picking up odd jobs where he could find them. He was good with engines and could fix just about anything given a little time and a few spare parts to work with. Sparky had warmed to him the moment he arrived. The old tractor looked shabby and down-at-wheel, yet there seemed to be a deep understanding and kindness beneath his battered rusty panels.

Sparky looked around the workshop. Various bits of rusty machinery lay scattered all around, some in pieces on benches, some under old tarpaulins. A big silver spanner lay on the work-bench. Sparky looked at it and whistled. It was the most beautiful spanner he had ever seen. The shaft was long but perfectly balanced, the hand-finished grip inlaid with mother-of-pearl, the jaws bisected by a sure, sharp edge. It was a work of art, a real beauty. And it was heavy too! Sparky could hardly lift it.

'Here you go, Rex,' he gasped, struggling across from the bench.

'Thanks.' Rex took the spanner and deftly tightened a bolt, just so. He straightened up. 'That should do it.'

He closed the engine cowling, reached in and turned the key. The harvester roared into life.

'How's that feel?' he asked.

TRUCK**DOGS**

File No: 00228302

NAME: HERCULES

BREED/MAKE: Great Dane/Ore Truck
COLOUR: Grey cab, yellow tray
IDENTIFYING MARKS: Red/white safety bars on side walls
TEMPERAMENT: Headstrong

FILE INFO:
14 years old. No fixed address. Whereabouts of parents unknown. Self-styled leader of Mongrel Pack street gang. Problem with authority. Tends to be bossy.

SPECIFICATIONS:
Engine: 12-cylinder, water-cooled turbo
Power Output: 735kW at 2100rpm
Fuel Requirements: Diesel (direct injection), hi-carb dog food with regular calcium top-up
Maintenance: monthly flea drench. Auto-worming System (AWS) standard. No service req.

'Much better,' said the collie, stretching and revving a little. 'Feels great! Many thanks.' He rolled off up the street. Rex nodded in satisfaction.

'I wish I could do that,' said Sparky.

Rex looked at him. 'You could learn.'

Sparky's tail wagged eagerly. He wanted to be a mechanic more than anything in the world. Maybe even more than being a member of the Mongrel Pack.

'I want to learn how to grind out cylinder heads and recondition gearboxes and –'

'Whoa there,' laughed Rex. 'Let's start with looking after your tools. Do you own a spanner?'

But before Sparky could answer, a horn beeped announcing the arrival of a customer at the pump. Rex holstered his own spanner and went outside. Sparky looked out and recoiled. It was Farmer Howell.

'Morning,' said Rex.

'Hrmph,' said Farmer Howell. 'Fill it up. Regular.'

He released his fuel cap with a little pop of pressure from within and looked sidelong at Rex. 'So you're the new mechanic, eh? Planning on staying long?'

Rex flipped the nozzle off its hook and began to pump fuel. 'No plans.'

Farmer Howell grunted as he took on the tank load. Rex looked at him from under his brow and checked the pump. He added a little more, then stopped.

'Reckon that'll do.'

'I said, fill it up,' Farmer Howell growled. 'And give me a couple of cans of two-stroke as well.'

Rex continued to pump in silence for a while longer. He replaced the cap and crossed to the fuel shed near the workshop to get the cans of two-stroke, catching Sparky's eye as he did so. Sparky thought he saw the slightest raising of an eyebrow.

Farmer Howell grunted again as he adjusted himself, clearly uncomfortable with a full tank sloshing about inside. He had the unmistakable look of one about to pass wind. Sparky shrank back into the workshop and closed his air vents.

Just then, Mr Scratchly rolled up at the pump, stopping with a jerk. He looked around impatiently, then took the nozzle and began to serve himself, first checking that the pump was working by squirting some fuel on the ground. It splashed around the pump and trickled towards Farmer Howell.

Farmer Howell was meanwhile looking more and more uncomfortable, clearly working up to a real beauty. Sparky's eyes widened in horror. Rex locked the fuel shed and glanced back towards Sparky. He saw the look in Sparky's eyes and turned around, instantly registering the spilt fuel and Farmer Howell's look of discomfort.

Rex hurled himself at Mr Scratchly, grabbing the nozzle and knocking him clear across the garage forecourt. At the same time he spun Farmer Howell around with his rear wheels so the pick-up's backside pointed out across the street. A second later a huge tongue of flame shot out of Farmer Howell's exhaust pipe, accompanied by a loud bang. A clump of grass growing by the roadside went up in flames.

Rex turned and sent his silver spanner flying towards the pump. It flashed in the sun as it spun through the air, locked onto the fuel-flow lever and flipped it around, turning it off.

Sparky looked on, open-mouthed. He hadn't even had time to bark.

'What in Dog's name do you think you're doing, you cwrazy halfbwreed?' cried Mr Scratchly.

A crowd began to gather. He turned to them, fumbling with his hearing aid. 'Darn twractor went and attacked me!'

'Got rabies by the looks of him,' said Edna Fleasome from amongst the onlookers. 'Thought so the minute he arrived in town. He's got shifty eyes.'

'Shifty eyes,' said Ida.

Rex retrieved the spanner and headed back towards the workshop. 'Flames and fuel don't mix,' he said as he went. 'Basic safety.'

Farmer Howell looked guilty.

Mr Scratchly called out after Rex. 'I'll be pwressing charges, you hear? I'll . . . I'll have you put down!'

'Then we won't have a mechanic again,' said Mr Dogsbody dryly. 'A town has to have a mechanic, you know. Who'll run the petrol station? Windy Howell? Now that would be asking for trouble.'

The others chuckled. Farmer Howell went red.

'I could run it,' said Mr Barker the storekeeper in a low voice that no one heard.

'That was amazing!' said Sparky as Rex rolled back into the workshop. 'How'd you do that?'

Rex didn't answer. He carefully wiped the spanner, checking the barrel and closing the jaws. Then he spun it with the ease of a practised tool-slinger and holstered it snugly by his rear wheel. Sparky was deeply impressed.

Rex's off-side rear hubcap fell off with a clang and rolled into the dirt, somewhat undermining the moment.

Rex sighed. He retrieved the hubcap and hung it on a nail outside the door next to the 'Open' sign.

'I'm falling apart.'

He looked out the side window at the dispersing crowd and shook his head. 'I don't need this kind of aggravation.'

'You're not leaving, are you? You only just got here.'

Rex was silent.

'I don't want you to go,' said Sparky. 'You're my friend. I haven't really got any others.'

Rex thought for a moment, then turned back to Sparky with a half-smile.

'You and me both.'

The next day dawned as hot as ever. The corrugated-tin roofs sizzled and popped in the heat and the old peeling paint on the verandah posts curled, hard and brittle. The few Truck-Dogs who ventured out stayed in the shade of the verandahs, squinting their eyes against the glare. Even the buzzing Truck-Bugs kept to the shady side of the street.

Prudence, Digger, Zoe and Hercules were kicking an empty oil can around in the main street, outside the general store. The can made a terrific amount of noise, clanging off the water troughs, whanging off the guttering and kerthunking off the wooden verandah posts as they whacked it with their wheels and bumper bars.

Mr Scratchly winced at the racket as he went past.

Bullworth stood with his big mouth open wide, opposite the store. He was the goals.

Sparky watched from across the street as the others played, following every move, waiting for the can to come his way.

Digger had the can. He dribbled around Zoe and was about to pass it to Prudence when Hercules thumped into him and sent him sprawling. The big ore truck lined up Bullworth and flicked the can skilfully with his front wheel, sending it spinning into his open mouth.

'Good shot, Herc!' cried Zoe. 'One, nil.'

Bullworth spat the can out onto the ground and felt around his back teeth with his tongue. 'Ow. Not so hard.'

'How about a free kick for shoving?' said Digger.

'That wasn't shoving. It was a nudge,' said Hercules. 'You wanna see a shove?'

'Save it,' said Digger.

Prudence flipped the can back into play with a shrug of her fender. Digger slewed sideways and smacked the can with his back hoe. Hercules was ready but the can glanced off Zoe's mixer and popped up into the air, over his roof. Quick as a flash Sparky jumped – straight up in the air like little dogs do – and caught the can in his teeth.

'Hey, way to go, Sparky,' said Prudence.

'Nice leap,' nodded Digger.

'Yeah, nice,' said Hercules. 'Just watch I don't squash you by mistake, okay?' He put a heavy wheel on Sparky's roof and pressed him right down on his springs.

'Yeah, okay,' said Sparky with difficulty. 'I'll watch out.'

He passed the can up to Hercules. The big truck let him go and the game continued. Sparky sat down again.

Rex, who was on his way to pick up some supplies, stopped under the store verandah and watched. He smiled as he remembered playing similar games long ago when he was a pup. The can clanged down nearby and he bent to retrieve it.

But Hercules was quickly there. 'Make way, old-timer. You'll do a gasket if you're not careful.'

Hercules flipped the can up into the air with his front wheel, spun around and caught it in his tray. He pointed at

Rex, then at the can – 'Old dog, new trick.' He winked and drove off, looking to the others for their approval.

Rex watched him go with a slight smile. Sparky looked from Rex to Hercules, then back again, amused and puzzled. He knew what Rex was capable of.

The can was back in play again.

'Keep that mouth open wide, big boy,' Prudence called to Bullworth. 'I'm about to level the score!'

'Caregul og ny teeg, okay?'

Prudence whacked the can with her tail, sending it rocketing into Bullworth's mouth. It hit the firewall at the back of his mouth and went straight down his gullet.

Bullworth's eyes bulged. 'Euuurgch. Helg! I'g chokngg!'

The others looked on.

'I think he's choking,' said Zoe.

'Yup, looks like it,' said Digger. He came up behind Bullworth and squeezed the big dozer's undercarriage with his back hoe.

'Yeeeee!' squealed Bullworth. The can shot out of his mouth, straight across the street, over Sparky's head, and smashed through the window of the general store.

'Whoops,' said Prudence. 'Time to go.'

'Do we get extra points for that?' asked Digger.

Mr Barker was outside in a flash. 'You hoodlums!' he cried.

'Sorry,' said Prudence with an apologetic shrug. 'Accidents happen.'

'Accidents?' yelled the storekeeper. 'You brats are the accidents! You did that on purpose!'

They began to protest but to no avail.

'This town would be a better place without mongrels like you,' snapped Mr Barker.

'Come on,' said Hercules to the others, turning his back and heading up the street. 'You're wasting your breath.'

'It was an accident,' said Rex quietly as the Mongrel Pack drove off.

Mr Barker turned on Rex. 'You keep out of this! Those mutts are nothing but vandals. Vandals and delinquents!'

'No, they're just kids.'

Mr Barker looked at the old tractor with narrow, bigoted eyes. He saw a scruffy hobo, a drifter with an unknown past and no future. A troublemaker.

'You're no better than they are,' he spat. As he turned back to the store, his eyes fell on Sparky.

'You again! I might have known. Well, your mother is going to hear about this!'

Later, Sparky found himself once again in Mrs Plugg's office.

'. . . and if I catch you messing about with that Mongrel Pack again, you won't be moving from your room for a week! Do you understand?'

NAME: PRUDENCE

BREED/MAKE: Dachshund/Fuel-Tanker Road Train
COLOUR: Black and tan
IDENTIFYING MARKS: Small birthmark on front left wheel arch
(Oh yeah, and she's really, really long)
TEMPERAMENT: Ironic

FILE INFO:
13 yrs. Address: longdoggy@woofermail.com
Parents separated. (Mother resides Combustion City. Father's whereabouts unknown.) Member of Mongrel Pack.

SPECIFICATIONS:
Engine: 8-cylinder, water-cooled
Power Output: 250kW at 2000RPM
Trailers: 3 x 12.5m general purpose tankers
Fuel Requirements: Multi-fuel capacity, regular dog food
Maintenance: 12-mth grease, oil change & good scratch on belly

Sparky winced.

'It –'

'I don't care if it wasn't your fault,' she said. 'You were there with them and you shouldn't have been. They are a bad influence. Do I make myself clear?'

Sparky hung his head. 'Yes, Mum.'

Mr Barker looked on smugly from one side of the desk. Mrs Plugg's eyes flickered in distaste. She had never much liked the storekeeper.

'The cost of fixing the window will be reimbursed,' the Mayor told him coolly, 'out of miscellaneous street repairs.'

Mr Barker nodded, satisfied, and departed.

Mrs Plugg looked at Sparky and her tone softened. 'Just try to keep out of trouble, all right? I know I'm a little hard on you sometimes.' Her glance fell for a moment on the photo of Mr Plugg. 'Go on now.'

Sparky headed off.

Mayor Plugg's face was a mixture of exasperation, concern and despair as she watched him go.

A week later the Mongrel Pack were hanging around Memorial Park. The statue of Lord Hubcap stared out at the windmill from behind its rope fence. There was some shade under the big spreading gum trees that were scattered through the park but the TruckDogs weren't concerned about keeping cool. They were doing time trials on the circular gravel path that ran around the statue.

Sparky looked on from across the road, his mother's words still ringing in his ears. He made a sad sight, sitting there, tail wagging occasionally as one of the Pack did a particularly good lap. He was dying to join in. He was trying to be good.

'Whoa, steady there, oh great leader,' called Prudence as Hercules roared around the track. 'You're going to cause a dust storm.'

'One lap to go,' called Zoe, checking his time on her trip computer.

Hercules put on a burst of speed, sending gravel and stones flying. Bullworth flinched. 'Ow, you're chipping my paintwork!'

Hercules completed the lap and skidded to a stop. Zoe checked the time. 'Thirteen point seven seconds. You're just the best, Herc!'

Hercules did a lap of honour. Zoe grabbed onto his rear bumper with her grille. 'C'mon, everyone. Conga line!'

Digger fell in behind Zoe with a happy 'Woo hoo', dragging Bullworth after him with his back hoe. They slewed from side to side alarmingly.

'This is going to end in tears,' said Prudence. But she shrugged and joined in anyway.

The conga line got faster and faster, spinning round and round the statue. Sparky watched, his tail thumping the ground in excitement. Unable to contain himself any longer, he bolted across the road, leapt the corner of the rope fence and began racing around behind them, unnoticed.

But in his excitement he didn't see that the rope had snagged on his rear axle. The rope tore away from the old posts, one after the other, but the last one held fast. The rope went tight for a second, then the post broke off. It flew inward, glancing off Bullworth's head, and smashed into the statue. One of Lord Hubcap's concrete ears went flying, never to be seen again. The rest of the head spun through the air and hit the ground with a thud, ten metres away.

Sparky was flung high into the air. He landed in the fork of an overhanging tree and hung there, wheels dangling, looking very surprised.

The Mongrels came to a stop, bumping into each other like shunting trucks as they became tangled up in the rope.

'Ow!'

'Ugh!'

'Ooof!'

'What happened?'

'Yeowwwwww!' cried Bullworth. A large welt had appeared on his head, surrounded by bare metal where the orange paint had come off. Tears welled in his eyes.

'Get this off me,' said Hercules, revving angrily against the rope that had wrapped itself around his wheels. There was a loud crack from above. The TruckDogs looked up to see the statue teetering on its base. Bullworth stopped in mid-sob, mouth open.

They watched, transfixed, as the statue teetered back and forth, working its way to the edge where it balanced for an impossibly long moment. Then, like a felled tree, it toppled earthward.

'Watch out!' yelled Prudence.

Zoe scrambled out of the way with a yelp as it crashed down. A cloud of cement dust billowed out over the park, coating everything in a layer of white.

Slowly the cloud cleared. The Mongrel Pack emerged coughing and spluttering. They looked like ghosts, completely white with dust. Prudence turned on her windscreen wipers and looked around.

'Er, guys,' she said. 'We have company . . .'

The others washed their windscreens, blinked and looked up. They did indeed have company. The entire population of the town in fact.

Mayor Plugg came forward and surveyed the broken statue in silence. Eventually she spoke.

'Is my son here?'

Up in the tree, Sparky bit his lip.

'No, just us,' shrugged Prudence.

The Mayor sighed. That was something at least. She looked at the statue, then squarely at the Pack.

'This is not an isolated incident,' she said sternly. 'You are

fast becoming a public nuisance. And that's something this town can do without.'

'They broke my window,' put in Mr Barker. 'They're vandals.'

'They've been worrying my sheep,' said Farmer Howell.

'They're rude and noisy,' said Mr Scratchly.

'Impudent!' exclaimed Edna Fleasome. 'Impudent and far too young.' She looked at her sister. 'Isn't that right, Ida?'

Ida hesitated. She vaguely remembered being young herself once, but she nodded. If Edna said so, then it must be right.

'Too young.'

'Quite a list,' remarked Digger.

'They left out "bored to death" and "totally lacking in opportunity",' remarked Prudence. 'But otherwise that just about covers it.'

'All right, yes, thank you,' said Mayor Plugg to the towns-folk. 'Please let me deal with this.'

'No, no, they've done a great job,' said Hercules. 'You don't want us here. And we don't want to be here. So fine. We're leaving.'

Prudence raised her eyebrows. 'And where would we be going exactly?'

'Anywhere but here.'

'Wait,' said Mayor Plugg. This wasn't what she had meant to happen. As Mayor of Hubcap she had a duty to maintain law and order, but she was also a mother. The Mongrel Pack some-times seemed practically adults themselves – with no proper homes they had grown up quickly – but in reality they were still just bored kids. She thought about Sparky, how he seemed to have nothing to do – nothing better than hang around with the Mongrel Pack. She frowned. They *were* a bad influence.

'Let 'em go,' snapped Mr Barker. 'We don't need 'em.'

Hercules turned and drove away across the park and out onto the street. He was followed by the others.

The townsfolk mumbled amongst themselves. Some, like Mr and Mrs Dogsbody, shook their heads worriedly. Others murmured their approval. A town had to have its standards.

'They need to be taught a lesson,' said Edna.

'At least my sheep will be safe,' said Farmer Howell.

'Maybe now we can all get a bit of peace and quiet,' said Mr Scratchly.

Farmer Howell backfired as he headed off.

'Not with him around,' remarked Mrs Dogsbody.

Mayor Plugg looked after the departing Mongrel Pack and didn't know what to think.

Rex was tinkering with an old gearbox, adjusting the tension with a screwdriver clenched between his old yellow teeth, when Sparky rushed into the workshop.

'They've gone!' gasped Sparky. 'The Mongrel Pack. I don't believe it.'

Rex put down his spanner. He followed Sparky to the door

and looked out across the desert, squinting into the sun. He scanned the horizon, but all he could see was the faintest shimmer of a dust cloud out towards the west.

Sparky told him what had happened.

'Those young hotheads are going to get themselves killed,' the old tractor muttered. 'There are DesertDogs out where they're heading.'

He looked for a while longer, then shook his head and turned back to the town. He spoke softly, as if reciting:

'A town that turns away its youth,

Will surely turn to dust.

And all that's left is fleas'n'weeds,

Some memories – and rust.

'I'm an old dog, Sparky. I've seen a lot of towns slowly fade away, eaten up from within, until there's nothing left but rust and resentment. I don't want to see any more.'

He flipped a saddle pack off its hook with a shrug of his wheel arch, and swung it up across his cab. He cast an eye around the workshop. 'Never did finish that gearbox,' he murmured regretfully.

'If you're leaving, I'm coming with you,' said Sparky.

Rex looked at the youngster and saw the lower lip jutting out, stubborn but trembling ever so slightly.

'You're young,' he said kindly. 'Believe it or not, I was once a pup myself. It was a long, long time ago. But I still remember. So I understand how you feel.'

He took down a couple of waterbags, and his tool kit and the big silver spanner. 'But a TruckDog should stay put as long as he has a job to do, a kennel to lie in and a bone to gnaw on.

'And unless I'm mistaken, there're a few more bones here for you to dig up yet, young fella – maybe more than you know. As for me . . .' He spun the spanner and slipped it into his tool kit and trundled off down the hill.

'Are you coming back?' called Sparky.

Rex paused. He didn't look back. 'You take care.'

He left the road and headed off across the desert, westward.

Sparky turned despondently to the workshop. He pushed the big doors closed. There, hanging on a nail next to the 'Open' sign, was Rex's old hubcap. Sparky looked at it for a moment, then hung his head.

Then with a sad shrug he turned the sign around to 'Closed'.

TRUCK DOGS

Reg No. 436861 42

NAME: BULLWORTH

BREED/MAKE: Bulldog/Bulldozer
COLOUR: Safety Orange
IDENTIFYING MARKS: Blue eyes, blue collar, big mouth
TEMPERAMENT: Surprisingly timid considering size

FILE INFO:
13 yrs. No fixed address. Parents deceased. Member of Hubcap street gang 'The Mongrel Pack'.

SPECIFICATIONS:
Engine: 4-stroke cycle, water-cooled, direct injection
Power Output: 300 kw at 1800rpm (flywheel horsepower)
Operating Weight: 15,200 kg and growing
Fuel Requirements: Diesel, oil and cabbages (note: vegetarian, no bones please)
Maintenance: 6 month: Oil & worm. 12 month: Flea powder

BITE TWO

Rex chugged slowly and steadily through a harsh landscape dotted with low, rounded boulders. Brittle bushes and clumps of dry grass grew close to the rocks where there was some shelter from the relentless sun. He scanned the ground as he went, looking for tyre tracks, but there were few signs to be read in the hard, stony ground.

Late in the afternoon he came to a billabong. A solitary gum tree stood with its gnarled branches hanging out over the pool. The water level was low. A few thirsty TruckRoos hopped away as he approached. Rex looked at the tree and noticed a small branch hanging down – freshly broken. Tyre prints were visible by the water's edge. He looked out to the west. The Mongrels were nowhere in sight. But he knew he was on the right track.

Rex filled his waterbags and topped up his radiator, rolling right into the billabong to find deeper water. Just then he heard the sound of engines approaching. Lots of engines. He reversed out of the water and waited quietly under the shade of the tree.

Soon the thunder of engines was so loud it made the surface

of the billabong shimmer. Over a low rise, coming out of the north, appeared twenty or so huge, aggressive-looking TruckDogs. They were a mangy lot, flecked with rust and spattered with mud. Some were standard models – utes mostly, a few twin cabs and tray trucks. Others were weird hybrids, sporting modifications of various kinds. Oily black smoke spewed from unsilenced exhaust pipes and boiling water dribbled from slavering grilles and overheated radiators.

They were the RottWheelers – a bunch of highway bandits and car thieves, led by the meanest TruckDog that ever hit the highway – the notorious Mr Big.

Each vehicle was loaded with supplies – spare parts, maintenance equipment, tyres. Some towed tarpaulin-covered trailers. They looked hot and tired but there was no sign they were going to stop at the billabong. They were driving hard.

Rex stood quietly under the gum tree as they passed, his dull, rusty panels blending in with the rocks and red earth. Most of the band had thundered by when one spied him and shouted an order. The other RottWheelers came about, tyres squealing, gearboxes crunching, and circled round the billabong to where Rex stood.

The sharp-eyed one was a greyhound/drag car with off-road wheels and suspension, powered by a rear-mounted aircraft-style ramjet engine. She was flame red with a wide yellow stripe down the roof and bonnet. Her grille was styled in a permanent sneer. Her name was Throttle. She was Mr Big's lieutenant.

'Hey, Brake, come and look at this.'

An enormous mastiff/monster truck came up beside her. Patches of bright electric blue showed through the mud that was spattered over his huge frame. He had a lot of amateur paint detailing on his door panels and multiple piercings on his wing mirrors and wheel arches. A heavy black leather collar with silver studs was fastened tightly around his girth and he sported gigantic tyres meant for a vehicle several times his size. But for all his bulk, Brake had a teeny weeny cab. Definitely not the brightest car in the auto pool.

Throttle nodded towards Rex, who remained motionless, eyes averted. 'Is this pile of junk dead or alive?'

'You want I bite it and find out?' said Brake in a guttural growl.

'Sure, go ahead. Course, it might be poisonous. Or rotten. Certainly looks flyblown.'

Brake thought for a minute, then grunted. 'I bite it anyway.'

But as he rolled forward another voice broke in, altogether smoother, infinitely more unpleasant. 'Thank you, Brake. That won't be necessary.'

The crowd of slavering TruckDogs parted and a little chihuahua/Isetta rolled forward. Apart from being one of the smallest TruckDogs ever conceived, he was also clearly one of the nastiest. He had a nasty face, all pinched and sneering – nasty thin lips, nasty buggy eyes and nasty little pointy teeth. And he was painted a particularly nasty shade of blue, too.

This was Mr Big.

He regarded Rex with distaste, then extended his antenna and, from a safe distance, poked the tractor sharply in the side. Rex remained motionless. Mr Big leaned forward and sniffed at him. It was a nasty sniff.

'Well, it certainly smells dead. But you can never tell with these old strays.' He turned to Throttle. 'Maybe he just needs a wash?'

Throttle grinned. 'You got it, Boss.'

She kicked out suddenly with her rear wheels, sending Rex sprawling into the billabong.

'Clean him up, boys.'

The RottWheelers drove into the billabong, hooting and hollering. They circled Rex, churning up the water, covering him in mud, then emptied his waterbags over his cab.

'That will do,' said Mr Big. The RottWheelers stopped obediently.

Rex groaned slightly as he lifted himself upright, flexing a dented wheel arch.

'Well, well – he's alive after all,' said Mr Big. 'What a shame we can't stay and play longer. Relieve him of his tools, Throttle my dear, and we shall be off. We still have a way to go.' He turned to Brake. 'What's the name of the next lucky town?'

Brake produced a map, unfolding it clumsily (his thick tyre tread pattern wasn't designed for such work), and read slowly. 'Uh, pacbuH.'

'And if we turn the map up the other way?'

'Er, Hubcap.'

Throttle rummaged through Rex's tool kit with her snout, discarding most of the tools – nothing but worthless old junk – but she eyed the spanner with interest.

'Now that's a nice tool.'

Rex's eyes flickered.

'Your spanner?' she asked.

Rex nodded.

'Not any more.' She stowed it in her tool compartment.

At that moment Mr Big rallied the RottWheelers, whipping the closest rump with his antenna. 'Let's ride!'

They revved their engines, a huge confusion of sound and smoke, and thundered off. Throttle circled Rex.

'Have a nice day now.' She gave him a wink and followed the others.

Rex hauled himself out of the water and watched as they disappeared towards the east. After a long moment he looked west, in the direction the Mongrel Pack were headed, as if judging the distance. He paused, weighing things up. Then he collected his other tools from where they lay scattered on the ground, wiped them clean, refilled his waterbags and set off after the Mongrel Pack.

The spanner would have to wait for later.

Sparky sat by himself in Hubcap Memorial Park, glumly contemplating the statue of Lord Hubcap lying in the dirt. The head lay some way off, looking rather surprised. A little TruckPuppy out with his mother strained at the leash to sniff at it. He lifted a wheel. His mother hastily dragged him away, scolding. Sparky laughed hollowly.

'Go for it, kid.'

Just then, the roar of engines filled the air. Sparky lifted his head, filled with a sudden hope. Was it the Mongrel Pack coming back? And Rex?

The cause of the commotion came into view, and his hope turned to sudden interest and then, just as quickly, alarm, as twenty huge TruckDogs came rumbling into town.

The townsfolk hurried inside, drawing blinds and bolting doors, as the cavalcade rolled up the main street.

Mr Big pulled in at the petrol station and looked around. Under the 'Closed' sign on the workshop wall hung another, reading, 'Mechanic Wanted'.

Mr Big sounded his horn. There was no response. The other RottWheelers joined in, circling the garage forecourt, honking and beeping. Eventually a very nervous-looking Mr Barker emerged from the general store, hurried down the street and across to the petrol station.

'Er, can I help you?'

Brake stuck his big grille right in the storekeeper's face. 'You delivery boy, huh?'

TRUCK DOGS

NAME: ZOE

BREED/MAKE: Dalmatian/Cement Mixer
COLOUR: Peacock blue with mauve highlights
IDENTIFYING MARKS: Lots of beauty spots
TEMPERAMENT: Sassy

FILE INFO:
12 yrs going on 18. No address, no parents. Mongrel Pack member. Often seen parking with Hercules (file 00228302).

SPECIFICATIONS:
Engine: 6-cylinder, d/i
Power Output: 112kW at 2300 rpm
Fuel Requirements: Something nice, preferably unleaded
Maintenance: Monthly wax, polish and fur-cleanse. Weekly tyre trim and windscreen de-bug (no harm in dreaming!)

Mr Barker blinked nervously. 'No, actually I own the general store. I'm looking after the garage until –'

Throttle grabbed him by the collar and spun him around to face her. 'Can you pump petrol?'

Mr Barker nodded meekly.

'So pump.'

He looked around at the assembled RottWheelers. 'Which one?'

Mr Big rolled up and tapped him on the cab with his antenna. 'All of us, Mr Delivery Boy. All of us. You can start with Brake here. He takes his unfiltered with plenty of lead.'

Brake loomed over Mr Barker, grinning. Mr Barker reached for the fuel nozzle but hesitated. Mr Big looked at him with narrowed eyes and smiled to himself – he'd seen this type before. He retracted his antenna, came alongside and spoke confidingly.

'You're a smart one, I can see that. You and I are not as different as you think. We all need fuel. And we all need friends – preferably big, powerful ones.'

Mr Barker's eyes flicked across to the RottWheelers and back. Mr Big raised an eyebrow. 'We understand one another, yes?'

The storekeeper swallowed. Just at that moment Mayor Plugg arrived.

'Ah, the official welcoming committee,' said Mr Big. '. . . numbering exactly one. Tell me, where is everyone else? Come out, come out, wherever you are!'

Mr and Mrs Dogsbody and a handful of the more stalwart townsfolk appeared and gathered behind Mrs Plugg. A few others emerged timidly, staying near their doors, keeping their distance.

'That's better,' said Mr Big. 'Come in closer now. We're not going to bite, you know.'

'Heh, heh, heh,' chuckled Brake.

The townsfolk shuffled their wheels, and kept their distance.

Mayor Plugg came forward and cleared her throat. She smiled in what she hoped was a friendly but firm way.

'Good afternoon to you all. And welcome to Hubcap. Is everything all right? If it's fuel you need, you only have to say. I am sure we can spare enough to see you on your way.'

Mr Big feigned surprise. 'Really? Why, that would be wonderful, wouldn't it, boys? The kind people here will let us have some of their precious fuel – "enough to see us on our way".'

Throttle smirked.

Mayor Plugg pressed on. 'You will understand, of course, that we're only a small town with limited supplies . . .'

'Well, that's going to be a problem, isn't it?' interrupted Mr Big. 'You see, lady, we're not here for "enough to see us on our way". We're here for "all that we can take"!'

Mayor Plugg bristled. 'Now listen here, just because there are a lot of you . . .' She looked around. 'Quite a lot of you – it doesn't mean you can just roll into town and take over.'

'Actually,' smiled Mr Big, 'it does.'

He clicked his door handles and several RottWheelers instantly lunged forward and sideswiped Mrs Plugg, wrapping a rope around her bonnet and tying it off on the roof-racks. Others attached heavy wheel clamps to her wheels. Throttle tightened them with the big silver spanner.

Brake bit the lock off the workshop doors and Mayor Plugg was shunted roughly inside.

'Now just a minute –' started Mr Dogsbody, the mobile crane moving forward, but he too was instantly grabbed, bound and hurled into the workshop.

'You leave him alone!' cried his wife, the scissor-lift. Then 'Ow! You leave *me* alone!' And she soon joined her husband.

Mr Big looked around at the stunned townsfolk. 'Anyone else?'

From the back of the group came a voice. 'Yeah. Me.'

It was Farmer Howell.

A pair of RottWheelers made to tackle him but he was ready for them. Before they knew what was happening he reared up on his back wheels, grabbed them in his front wheels and banged their cabs together. They staggered away, reeling. Farmer Howell turned to face Mr Big. The little Isetta held his antenna out in front of him and put himself into reverse.

'Keep him away from me!'

The other RottWheelers, led by Throttle and Brake, piled onto Farmer Howell. The crusty old pick-up put up a good fight, giving several of the thugs dents they would long remember, but there were too many for him. Soon he was trussed and clamped and thrown in the workshop with the others.

Mr Big looked again at the townsfolk. 'Anyone? Anyone at all?'

The townsfolk hung their heads.

Satisfied, Mr Big turned to Mr Barker. The storekeeper lifted the fuel nozzle off its hook and held it up in readiness. But Throttle snatched it from him.

'Forget it, Delivery Boy. We prefer self-service.'

She smashed the pump's glass window with Rex's spanner and, pointing the nozzle skyward, shot a fountain of fuel high up into the air.

'It's party time! Yeeeha!'

The RottWheelers honked and revved, pushing and shoving to get at the free petrol. Suddenly a flash of white and brown flew through the air, snatching the nozzle from the unsuspecting Throttle.

Sparky landed squarely on his wheels, bristling and growling, his jaws clamped around the nozzle.

'This is our fuel,' he said through clenched teeth. 'And this is our town. And that . . .' he nodded towards the workshop doors, 'is my mum! Now you let her go or . . . or . . .'

He looked around at the huge and very unfriendly thugs who had encircled him. The rush of fuel to his carburettor subsided. Mr Big rolled forward and relieved him of the nozzle.

'Or what? You'll nip me on the axle?' He tapped Sparky with his antenna. 'You are a naughty puppy. And naughty puppies need to be disciplined.'

He motioned to Throttle. She pulled the tarpaulin cover off one of the trailers. Underneath was a big iron cage. And inside the cage was a monster.

From the sloping bonnet that began almost at the roof-line, it appeared to be a bull terrier/heavy-haulage hybrid but it was hard to tell for sure. The rear-drive wheels were enormous. A huge engine protruded from behind the cab, the exhaust stack sticking up vertically from the block. Wild albino eyes stared out from a heavy leather-and-steel muzzle.

Throttle pulled the bolt on the cage door. The monster sprang out with a roar and hurled itself at Sparky, who stood rooted to the spot. But suddenly the beast gave a choked yelp, pulled back in midair by a heavy chain attached to the cage. It landed with a solid thud but immediately scrabbled to its wheels again and began barking insanely at Sparky, pulling at the end of its chain.

Mr Big tapped the monster on the nose with his antenna. 'Clutch. Sit.'

Clutch looked at Mr Big, uncomprehending. Mr Big held up a Doggy Bite on the end of his antenna.

'Sit . . .' Clutch sat down.

'Good boy.' He flicked the Doggy Bite towards the monster. It vanished down its gullet in an instant.

Clutch looked up expectantly.

'Still hungry? Dear me, I seem to be out of Doggy Bites.' Mr Big half-turned and spoke confidingly to Sparky. 'You should run away now – it makes it so much more fun for him.'

Sparky looked with horror at the monstrous TruckDog. Long strings of oily saliva drooled from the leather-encased grille. Mr Big undid the strap at the back of Clutch's harness and let it fall to the ground. The steel muzzle remained, fixed in place by a pin. A thin string hung from the pin. Mr Big held it in the tread of his front wheel.

'Steady . . .'

Clutch remained sitting, eyes fixed on Sparky, shaking in anticipation.

Sparky backed away, fumbling to find reverse gear, then turned and fled. Mr Big waited until he had made it as far as the general store. Then he pulled the pin. The steel muzzle fell to the ground.

'Fetch.'

Clutch sprang away, howling.

Sparky knew his life was on the line. He could never out-run the massive beast. His only chance was his size. Quick as a flash, he scurried down the narrow space between the general store and the bone depot next door, his wing mirrors folded back so they didn't hit the walls. He reached the far end and glanced back.

Clutch flung himself headlong into the narrow space and

accelerated forward. There was a rending, screeching sound as he became wedged between the walls. He spun his wheels furiously, tearing up the dirt, but he was stuck fast.

Sparky poked out his tongue. Clutch roared in fury and surged forward, bringing half the store wall with him in an avalanche of splintered weatherboards and corrugated iron.

Sparky fled up the lane, back into the main street and across into Memorial Park. An instant later Clutch roared round the corner in pursuit.

Sparky was breathing hard. He couldn't keep running much longer. He saw Lord Hubcap lying headless in the dirt. He glanced up at the sheared-off base of the statue. Then Clutch was upon him. He scurried to the other side of the statue base. Clutch leapt after him. Soon they were racing round and round the path, throwing up a great cloud of white dust.

Sparky could hear Clutch roaring and snarling right behind him, but the dust cloud was so thick he couldn't see him. All at once he sprang up onto the statue base. Below him, Clutch continued to go in circles. After a few more laps the monster veered away, staggering dizzily, and thudded into a tree which shuddered at the impact. He shook his head violently to clear it and looked around.

Up on the concrete base Sparky froze, statue-like, under a thick coating of white dust. Clutch prowled about below him, growling, sniffing the ground.

Sparky's nose began to tickle. He started to sweat.

At last Clutch moved away, following Sparky's trail back across the park. Suddenly the sound of a muffled sneeze came from behind him. He spun back with a snarl. He looked up at the statue. A faint cloud of dust floated above it. Clutch cocked his head quizzically to one side. Sparky remained absolutely motionless.

Then, with a grunt, Clutch looked around the park again. His prey was nowhere in sight. With a bark of frustration he roared away.

Sparky waited until he was sure the monster had gone. Then he blinked, jumped down and scurried off.

Far out in the baking desert, the Mongrel Pack were a long way from home. A merciless sun beat down upon their unprotected roofs. Their tongues were hanging out. Digger had excavated several holes as they went along, looking for water, but without success.

Bullworth was panting. 'My tracks are burning. I've got blisters on my drive wheels.'

'Try hopping on one track,' Prudence suggested. Bullworth tried but he couldn't keep his balance.

'Actually, I was only joking.'

'Can't we stop soon, Herc?' pleaded Zoe.

'Yeah. I'm starving,' said Digger. 'I haven't eaten for hours.'

File No: 00?...846

NAME: DIGGER

BREED/MAKE: Labrador/Back Hoe
COLOUR: Sort of dusty yellow
IDENTIFYING MARKS: Well, there is that big orange light on top of his head
TEMPERAMENT: Easy-going

FILE INFO:
Age: 12 yrs. Address: nup. Parents: Got a couple — just doesn't know where they are right now. Member of Mongrel Pack gang.

SPECIFICATIONS:
Engine: 4-cylinder, 3990 cc
Power Output: 84kW at 2600 rpm
Loader: Standard bucket (2270mm)
Lifting Capacity: 4400 kg
Fuel Requirements: Anything that's going
Maintenance: Nah

'You could try eating leaves and berries,' suggested Bullworth.

'If there were any,' added Zoe.

Hercules looked ahead and spied a rocky outcrop shimmering in the distance. 'We'll stop at those rocks. At least there'll be some shade.'

'You can't eat shade,' said Digger.

'Depends what's making the shadow,' remarked Prudence.

The outcrop was closer than it at first appeared. They were soon making their way between the rocks, clambering over them where necessary. Suddenly Hercules stopped and listened.

'Wait here,' he said to the others. 'Digger, come with me.'

Hercules and Digger crept quietly forward. The sound of growling and scuffling could be heard coming from somewhere not far ahead. They peeped out from behind a boulder to see an open, sandy area. A pool of water lay to one side, flanked by some trees. By its edge lay the dried-up remains of a wild TruckSheep. Digger licked his lips.

But around the carcass, gnawing on the bones, was a pack of dingo/4x4s. They were mainly old Land Cruisers and Patrols, single cabs with large bullbars and ragged, patched-canvas covers that hung from scrawny roll bars on their pick-up backs. They snarled and growled at each other as they fought over the carcass. There were seven or eight of them.

'DesertDogs,' whispered Hercules. 'Could be tricky.'

'Food,' said Digger, looking at the TruckSheep carcass and licking his lips again. 'Who cares?'

Hercules gazed at the carcass too and his gearbox rumbled. He thought for a moment.

'Okay, we're going to need a diversion.'

An old TruckSheep skull – just the bonnet, roof and front window frames – lay nearby.

'Grab that,' said Hercules. 'And let's get back to the others.'

'You've gotta be kidding!' said Bullworth as Digger and Hercules outlined the plan. 'We're talking DesertDogs here. They eat things like us for breakfast.'

'For once I'm with Bullworth,' said Prudence. Zoe nodded.

'Listen,' said Hercules. 'Without food we are going to die. It's a dog-eat-dog world out here.'

'Not an expression I would have used under the circumstances,' remarked Prudence dryly. 'But I guess you're right – we gotta eat. Lead on, oh great one.'

A little later the DesertDogs were gnawing away on the carcass, growling and snapping at each other, when something vaguely resembling a TruckSheep popped up from behind a rock on the far side of the clearing. It bleated, not very convincingly.

The DesertDogs looked up curiously. The TruckSheep bleated again and moved up and down a bit.

Behind the rock, Digger held up the TruckSheep skull with his back hoe, bobbing it up and down. The skull had been dressed up with some dried grasses and leaves which they hoped looked a little like wool from a distance.

Zoe was doing the bleating.

'I can't keep this up much longer,' gasped Digger. The skull was heavy and sweat was trickling into Digger's eyes.

'Baaa! Lift it up a bit more,' hissed Zoe. 'Not that much, your bucket's showing. Baaaaa!'

Behind a boulder further round the clearing Hercules, Prudence and Bullworth were watching. The DesertDogs left the carcass and went to investigate the decoy TruckSheep.

'Looks like they've swallowed it,' said Hercules.

'They'll swallow us if we're not careful,' remarked Prudence. But Hercules wasn't listening.

'Okay, you two . . . Go.'

Prudence and Bullworth edged away from the boulder and made their way around the back of the outcrop, coming up on the carcass from the far side. It was half buried in the sand. With a quick glance to be sure the DesertDogs were fully occupied with the fake TruckSheep, Prudence took one of the carcass's horns between her teeth and tugged. It didn't budge. Bullworth took the other horn. They pulled together. Nothing.

'A little harder,' said Prudence.

They pulled a little harder and the head came right off.

'Oh, great,' said Bullworth. 'Now we'll never get it out.'

At that moment they heard a low growl. They looked up to find a Desert Dog standing on a rock above them. Prudence and Bullworth grinned stupidly.

'Sorry, our mistake,' said Prudence. She replaced the head, arranging it neatly, and backed away. The DesertDog snarled, revealing a gleaming set of dagger-like incisors.

Bullworth and Prudence squealed and fled.

A short time later, Prudence and Bullworth stood huddled together within the ring of rocks, guarded by three ferocious-looking DesertDogs. They were soon joined by Digger and Zoe and Hercules. The TruckDogs were no match for the lithe and powerful desert-dwellers.

The leader, a big brute with one yellow eye and a scar that ran down his fender from windscreen to wheel well, came forward and regarded the captives greedily. His gaze fell on Bullworth and he licked his lips.

Bullworth's eyes grew wide. 'No no no,' he protested. 'I'm tough – all gristle and cogs. I'll taste terrible. I'm a *vegetarian*, for pity's sake!'

The leader advanced on the hapless dozer but suddenly a rock crashed down on his roof, leaving a large dent. He yelped in pain and surprise. Everyone looked up. Atop the rocky outcrop, sharply drawn against the westering sky, stood the dramatic silhouette of a TruckDog – a tractor with a wonky funnel.

'Sorry to have to do that,' called Rex, 'but I needed to get your attention. Now, I'd like you DesertDogs to leave these young pups alone and go back to your lawful business. They've no right to be here, I know, but they're no threat to you and they're no good to eat, seeing as they're not dead yet.'

The one-eyed leader snarled savagely and barked an order. The DesertDogs howled furiously and leapt up the rocks. Rex sighed and waited, immobile on the ridge. The leader lunged at him. Rex caught him by the scruff of the neck with his teeth and with one fluid motion threw the 4x4 behind him over the rocky ledge. The DesertDog disappeared with a yelp and a distant thud.

A second 4x4 came at Rex from the side. Rex raised a thin, sinewy front wheel. The DesertDog crunched into it as if it were made of iron. Rex took hold of the beast's nose between his front wheels and twisted sharply. The DesertDog flipped over with a surprised yelp and disappeared over the ledge.

Two more DesertDogs attacked. Rex spun around and struck out with front and back wheels together, catching one of them under the sump and sending it, wheels flailing, into a prickly mass of sagebrush. The other Dog soared off in the opposite direction into a rock face and crumpled to the desert floor, senseless.

The one-eyed leader reappeared behind Rex.

'Watch out!' cried Bullworth. Rex turned and faced the DesertDog, alert, ready.

The leader paused, and for a moment their eyes met. Then the DesertDog lowered his gaze and slunk away, limping, descending to the desert floor. He looked back at Rex with his one baleful eye. Then he barked an order and the DesertDogs dragged themselves upright and retreated, licking their wounds, into the desert.

The Mongrels watched them go, then looked back at Rex, gob-smacked.

Prudence broke the silence. 'Well, that was impressive.'

'Strewth!' enthused Digger. 'That was awesome! Who says you can't teach an old dog new tricks, eh, Herc?'

Hercules looked uncomfortable.

Rex clambered down to the desert floor. He rotated his left front wheel painfully.

'Old tricks. Even older dog.' He looked at Hercules and the others from under his eyebrows. 'You might need a few extra tricks yourselves if you're planning to stay out here for long.'

'Planning has not been high on the agenda so far,' said Prudence.

Zoe looked at Hercules. 'Can't we go home now, Herc?'

'We're not going back to Hubcap. They don't want us – and we don't need them. And we don't need your tricks either, Mr Mechanic. We can look after ourselves.'

'So I see,' said Rex. He looked up at the sky. 'Well, I'll be going, then. I for one don't plan to be out here when it gets dark. Those DesertDogs will be back, and in greater numbers. This is their territory, not ours.'

The TruckDogs glanced around, noticing the lengthening shadows. A distant, chilling howl came floating across the desert. Bullworth's eyes bulged. Prudence's hair stood on end all the way along the back of her trailers.

'Yeeesh! Now that's a sound you could learn to hate.'

She sidestepped across to where Rex stood. 'I'm with the tractor. No offence, Herc, but there's only so much abject terror a girl can take in one day.'

Bullworth, Zoe and Digger gulped nervously and gathered close together with Prudence.

'C'mon, Herc . . .' pleaded Zoe.

Another howl punctuated the night, closer this time and off to the left. Hercules struggled with himself, trying to be brave, wanting to act like a leader. But in reality he was scared too.

'Okay, so we find somewhere safe for the night.'

The others breathed a sigh of relief.

'But tomorrow we keep moving.'

The streets of Hubcap were deserted. The townsfolk had been ordered to stay indoors and RottWheelers patrolled the streets, growling ferociously at anyone who showed so much as a headlight.

The rest of the gang had made themselves at home in the workshop. Empty cans of engine oil and brake fluid lay scattered across the floor and more were being emptied at an alarming rate.

Mayor Plugg, Farmer Howell and Mr and Mrs Dogsbody sat bound and clamped at the back of the workshop, looking on helplessly as the gang gorged themselves on the precious fuel.

'Hey, Delivery Boy, more brake fluid,' called one RottWheeler.

A harried Mr Barker hurried across to the shelf.

'It's all gone.'

'Then go to the shed and get some more,' growled the RottWheeler.

'And a can of diesel,' added another.

'Two-stroke. Step on it!' ordered a third.

Mr Big looked on with a mixture of amusement and distaste as Mr Barker hurried off.

'It's a dog's life.'

Meanwhile, Sparky was sneaking along the back lanes of Hubcap, headlights off, engine just ticking over, towards the sound of the RottWheelers' celebration. There was a full moon (he suppressed the desire to howl), which cast an eerie blue light over the landscape. He came to a corner, peeped around and ducked back quickly as a RottWheeler patrol motored by.

TRUCKDOGS

NAME: REX

BREED/MAKE: Red Setter/Tractor

COLOUR: Used to be red

IDENTIFYING MARKS: Bald tyres, loose funnel, missing hubcaps, leaky exhaust, out of rego, no roadworthy — stuff that just happens when you've done that many kilometres

TEMPERAMENT: Quiet type

Reg No.
83845
v1

FILE INFO:

Age: can't remember exactly. Pretty old.

Address: c/o Hubcap Garage.

SPECIFICATIONS:

Engine type: 4-cylinder

Power Output: About 50hp last time he checked

Requirements: No preference

ance: Self-service

When they had passed he crept on to the workshop, slipping down the side of the building and round the back. The shadows were deep there, almost black. He wondered if he dared turn on his lights.

Suddenly he heard a noise. It sounded like a large bag of air being deflated. He stopped dead. It came again, then silence. Sparky remained motionless, straining to see. After a long while he decided to risk a little light. He flicked on his low beam – and nearly yelped in fright.

There, barely a metre from his nose, was the huge and unmistakable shape of Clutch. The monster was asleep, snoring, chained to a stake in the ground. An empty packet of Doggy Bites lay next to him. Slowly Sparky began to back away, eyes fixed on the sleeping beast. Clutch rolled over, drooling a long string of saliva, growled something unintelligible and belched right in Sparky's face.

Sparky gasped and staggered back into a sheet of corrugated iron that was leaning up against the wall. It fell with a clatter. Sparky froze. Clutch grunted and half opened a bleary eye, then slurped in the saliva, rolled over and fell back into another demented dream.

Inside the workshop, Throttle looked up. She had heard something. She nudged Brake, who was drinking noisily from a bucket.

'You hear something?'

'Huh? No. Nothing. Just this.' He slurped noisily again

from the bucket. Throttle whacked him on the back of the cab, dunking his snout in the fuel dregs. Brake spluttered angrily.

'Now, now, settle down,' said Mr Big. 'It was probably just Clutch pining. He's been a bad dog, letting that little mutt get away. But you know, I just can't see him suffer. Throttle, you can untie him now.'

'Okay, Boss.'

Mr Big turned to Brake, whose face was back in the bucket, and sighed.

'Try to use some manners, will you?'

Brake looked up quizzically, covered in slop. He had no idea what the boss was talking about.

Outside, Sparky gave Clutch a wide berth and snuck up to the back of the workshop. He sniffed along the wooden plinth until he found what he was looking for.

'Psst! Mum,' he whispered. 'Can you hear me?'

'Sparky, is that you?' whispered Mayor Plugg from the other side of the weatherboards.

'Move closer to the wall. I'm going to try to unlock your wheels.'

Mayor Plugg and the others shuffled carefully to the workshop wall, glancing nervously at the RottWheelers. But the RottWheelers were too busy with their refuelling to notice.

Sparky found a loose weatherboard. He flipped a tyre lever out of his tray and, holding the lever between his teeth, inserted it under the board.

Inside, one of the RottWheelers had flooded his carburettor and began misfiring noisily, much to the amusement of the others.

Sparky pressed down on the tyre lever, prising off the loose board. It squeaked and snapped but the sound was lost in the general noise of hooting and laughing inside.

He stooped down on his suspension and peered inside. He could see the captive's wheel clamps.

'Hold still . . .'

He poked his nose in as far as he could, a screwdriver clamped between his teeth, and by feel began to pick the locks on the wheel clamps, starting with Mr Dogsbody. Soon the left-hand pair were loose.

'Turn round.'

Mr Dogsbody wriggled around to face the other way. After a moment he was free. Next Mrs Dogsbody was released, then Farmer Howell. Sparky started work on Mayor Plugg.

'Sparky, where did you learn to do this?' she whispered.

'Hanging around with bad influences.'

He had three of Mayor Plugg's wheel clamps off and was working on the last when Throttle came round the corner, headlights on. Sparky was caught in the beam.

'Hey, you!' yelled Throttle.

Sparky released the last bolt, dropped the screwdriver and fled. He skidded round the corner and ran straight into Clutch, whose sleeping form now straddled the whole lane. The monster woke with a start, jumped up and looked groggily this way and that. He didn't have his muzzle on. Sparky stood right in front of him, horror struck. Clutch snarled and lunged forward, pulling the stake right out of the ground.

'ROOOOAAAAAR!'

At the same moment Sparky leapt past him with a yell that was an equal mix of terror and determination.

'YAAAAAH!'

Inside the workshop Mayor Plugg heard the commotion and instinctively cried out.

'Sparky!'

The RottWheeler gang looked around.

The unbolted wheel clamps lay on the ground for all to see.

'Run!' cried Mayor Plugg to the others. She quickly scooped up the screwdriver. The others made a dash for the door but it was blocked by a wall of snarling RottWheelers.

Mr Big rolled up to the captives. 'I am disappointed in you. I go out of my way to be reasonable – I don't kill anyone or burn the place to the ground – but then you try to escape. I'm afraid I shall now have to deal severely with you.'

'Lock them in the fuel shed,' he told Brake, then turned to Mr Barker. 'Keys please, Delivery Boy.'

Mr Barker glanced at Mayor Plugg, then held out a big

bunch of keys. Brake snatched them in his grille. Mayor Plugg held Mr Barker's eye as she and the others were led off.

He looked away.

'YAAAAAAAH!' cried Sparky.

'ROOOOAAAAARRR!' bellowed Clutch.

Sparky ran flat out, driving blind. He scurried around a corner into the main street. Clutch, free of his muzzle but with the chain flailing wildly behind him, was right on his tailpipe. Sparky could feel his hot breath. He nearly gagged at the smell.

But a full bag of Doggy Bites was having its effect on Clutch. He swung out wide on the corner, right through a verandah post. The heavy chain whipped around as he sped off, taking out the rest of the posts one after the other.

A moment later, Throttle came racing around the corner, just in time for the verandah to collapse on top of her in a mass of rubble.

Sparky raced past the old windmill. Digging in his wheels he made a tight curve around the water tank, and sped off again in the opposite direction. Clutch followed, wheels scrabbling, carving up a huge arc of dirt as he slewed out wide. The swinging chain smashed through a row of old sheds, reducing them to flying splinters and taking the top clean off a low-roofed TruckChicken roost. Startled

TruckChooks flew everywhere, squawking and flapping their wings.

Sparky tore up the road towards the 'Welcome To Hubcap' sign. But Clutch was gaining on him. The big beast was not good on corners but he was a lot faster than Sparky on the straight. His head was clearing and he had his prey in his sights now. Sparky was tiring, out of tricks, desperate. The monster bore down on him as they approached the sign.

Sparky could feel Clutch at his back. The terrible jaws opened, ready for the kill. At the last minute Sparky veered off the road onto the verge and ducked down on his springs under one of the big iron beams that flanked the sign. Clutch swerved to follow – and slammed headlong right into the beam with a sickening crunch. The heavy posts splintered and the iron beam rang like a bell as the vibrations ran up and down its length.

Clutch staggered back onto the road, eyes rolling up into his head. He fell sideways into a ditch by the roadside, a stupid smile across his face, and lay with his wheels in the air.

Sparky reversed back and sniffed at him gingerly. He was out cold. Sparky fixed the chain securely to the beam and scuffed up the grass – satisfaction at a job well done – then headed off back into town. As he passed by, he jumped up at the swinging sign.

And he hit it.

Mr Big watched as Brake and four burly RottWheelers re-clamped Farmer Howell and the Dogsbodys and pushed them roughly into the small fuel shed next to the workshop. A sign on the door read, 'Danger – Highly Inflammable – No Naked Flames'. Mrs Dogsbody looked at the sign with alarm.

'Mr Howell, you are going to have to control yourself.'

Farmer Howell nodded and gulped.

Mayor Plugg was being wheel-clamped when Sparky arrived, stealing up behind a bush, close enough to see and hear what was going on. He watched helplessly as Mrs Plugg was forced towards the shed.

'As lawfully elected Mayor of Hubcap I demand you release me and my companions immediately,' she said.

Brake looked at Mr Big questioningly.

Mr Big rolled his eyes. 'We're in charge here, you idiot. Don't listen to her.'

'Okay, Boss. Don't listen to her,' he told the others. They kept pushing Mrs Plugg towards the door. At that moment Throttle arrived.

'It was that little mutt again, Boss – the Mayor's son. But Clutch is after him.' She grinned nastily. 'He won't get away this time.'

'Sparky! No!' cried Mayor Plugg as she was pushed inside and the door slammed.

'Excellent,' said Mr Big. 'Now let's get rid of Mummy Dear.'

Mr Big produced a lighter and flicked it on. He held it out gingerly towards the shed with one wheel. Sparky's eyes grew wide. He was about to spring out when Throttle spoke.

'Hang on, Boss. This shed is loaded – it'll blow sky high.'

'That's the whole idea.'

'But it's gonna take the petrol station with it. It's too close. There's lots of fuel in those tanks yet.'

Mr Big considered this for a moment, then flicked the lighter off.

'You're right.' He turned to the RottWheelers. 'You four, guard this shed. We'll save the fireworks as a parting gift *after* we've relieved Mayor Plugg and her friends of all the fuel. And I mean *all* of it – every last drop.'

'Go and find something big to pump it into,' he told Throttle. 'Something really big. We're gonna squeeze this town dry.'

The four RottWheelers took up positions on each side of the shed as Mr Big motored off. Throttle turned to Brake.

'Okay, you heard him – something really big. Come on.'

They departed, leaving the other RottWheelers standing guard. From his hiding place Sparky looked on in despair. He cast around desperately – and saw the battered hubcap hanging on the workshop door.

'Rex . . .'

The sun had dipped below the horizon and the vast desert sky had begun to glow a deep indigo when Rex and the Mongrel Pack came to a sudden dip in the ground before them.

TRUCK**DOGS**

NAME: MAYOR PLUGG

BREED/MAKE: Irish Setter/Land Rover Discovery

COLOUR: Green with white stripe

IDENTIFYING MARKS: Mayoral Badge of Office

TEMPERAMENT: Stern but fair (she hopes)

FILE INFO:

Age: Confidential

Address: Mayoral Office, Hubcap Town Hall, HUBCAP, 0860

Tries to be fair and reasonable but is over-protective of son Sparky (file 00228301).

SPECIFICATIONS:

Engine: 8-cylinder, 5.2 Litre

Fuel Requirements: Unleaded petrol

Maintenance: As per service booklet

'Looks promising,' said Rex.

At first it seemed little more than a depression in the desert floor, but as they travelled along it became a rocky gully. The shadows grew deeper as they made their way downwards, the last light of the day fading from the sky. Suddenly the gully opened out into a broad hidden valley set below the level of the surrounding desert. The Mongrel Pack stopped and gaped. Before them lay a huge junkyard. Rusted-out vehicle hulks rested amongst ancient farm machinery, pumping equipment, traction engines and other old and broken contraptions. As night came on and the shadows grew into black pits, it looked very spooky indeed.

'So this is your idea of a nice safe place to spend the night, hey, Rex?' said Prudence. 'Very cosy. Love the graveyard theme.'

'I'd say it was the old tip from years back when Hubcap was still a thriving town. Hasn't been used in decades, by the looks of it. DesertDogs wouldn't come here. They'd think it was haunted.'

Prudence looked around at the twisted metal wreckage that loomed out of the twilight all around. 'You don't say.'

Hercules grunted and went on ahead of the others. He was being brave and silent, still smarting from the confrontation earlier that afternoon.

Bullworth and Zoe peered around at the junk and gulped. They crept forward nervously, winding their way between towering piles of contorted steel frames, warped and torn panels and rusting body parts.

The leering grille of an ancient Buick loomed out of the darkness, rubber pipes spilling out from the engine block like entrails, the windscreen gaping like an empty eye socket. A TruckRat scuttled out from behind the dashboard and disappeared into the darkness. Zoe screamed. Bullworth backed away, bumping into something behind him. He turned as the skull-like bucket of a huge old steam shovel tipped out towards him. Muddy water sloshed out of the shovel over his terrified face.

'Aaargh! Get it away from me!' he squealed.

Digger went up to the shovel and smiled. 'Don't worry, Bullworth. It's just my old Grandpa Fergus. He always was a bit of a dribbler.'

Prudence looked at the old steam shovel with a mixture of horror and curiosity.

'Your grandpa? You've got to be joking?'

Digger smiled wickedly and moved on. Prudence realised she'd been had. 'You *were* joking, you beast! I'm the one who says things like that, not you!'

But the mood had been lightened. They pressed on deeper into the valley, laughing as they came across old bits and pieces that reminded them of folk back in Hubcap.

'This one looks like Farmer Howell,' said Zoe, pointing at a large pick-up truck with a smashed-up rear end.

'Just as long as it doesn't smell like him,' said Prudence.

'Here's Mr Barker,' called Digger, coming across a particularly unappealing van. He worked the bonnet up and down from behind like a ventriloquist. 'You did that on purpose, you vandals! Yap yap yap, blah blah blah.'

'Put a lid on it will you?' growled Hercules, coming back. 'This stuff is nothing but trash – old junk, dead and gone.'

Rex raised his eyebrows and regarded him thoughtfully. 'Old, yes. Dead, maybe – but not gone.' A rusty pump engine stood nearby. 'That old heart has life in it yet.' He turned the flywheel and they could hear the pistons move inside the engine block.

He pointed at the heavy boiler plate of a huge traction engine. 'This steel is still strong.'

He ran his wheel over the blade of an old plough. 'The edge of these ploughshares still have work to do.'

'So what are you now, some kind of cosmic oriental mystico?' said Hercules. 'It's all just junk.'

Rex was silent. The others stood by uncomfortably.

Hercules snorted, breaking the silence. 'I've had enough of this. Come on, guys.'

He rumbled off towards the cleft leading up to the desert floor and looked back.

'I said, "Come on!" Am I the leader of the Pack or what? Are you going to stay and listen to Mr Deep-and-Meaningful here? You want to be the Cosmic Tractor Gang now, huh?'

The other TruckDogs looked at him unhappily. Rex spoke quietly.

'No, Hercules, they want to follow you. But you have to learn how to lead them.'

'What's that supposed to mean?' asked Hercules. 'Ah, just forget it.' And he stormed off. Zoe made to go after him but Rex gently restrained her.

'He needs a little time to work this out for himself. We can stop here for the night.'

Hercules had not gone far. He stood fuming by a tangled pile of steel reinforcing rods. Rocks that had fallen from the surrounding cliffs lay scattered amongst the steel rods. He stomped angrily on the edge of a rock, flipping it up into the air and catching it in his tray.

'It's a good trick,' said Rex, rolling up behind him. Hercules glanced at him, then looked away. Rex continued.

'You're a strong TruckDog, Hercules, and you're clever. But there are still things you can learn. A leader can always learn.'

'Yeah? Like what?'

'Like not forcing your friends to choose between their heads and their hearts,' said Rex sharply.

Hercules thought a bit and grunted. Rex went on more softly.

'Like not trying so hard to *act* like a leader – just *be* one. Make room for the others, Hercules. Everyone has their own role to play, their own talent. The smallest is as worthy of respect as the biggest.' He picked up a piece of junk, an old camshaft. 'And the old just as useful as the new.'

'And I thought you meant learn something practical,' said Hercules sullenly.

'Yes, practical is good, too.'

He pointed to a huge boulder with the camshaft. 'Flip that one up into your tray.'

Hercules looked at the rock, judging its weight. 'It's too heavy.'

'Throw it then,' said Rex casually. 'As far as you can. Over the junk pile.'

'Don't be ridiculous.'

Rex rammed the camshaft under the edge of the boulder, jumped into the air and came down hard on the end of the shaft, catapulting the rock high over the junk pile into the darkness beyond.

Hercules was impressed. But he tried not to show it.

'With your strength and ability you could learn to throw it twice as far,' said Rex. 'With a little help from this "junk" that you think so little of . . .'

Hercules looked around at the junk pile, then back at Rex. 'Okay,' he said. 'I'm listening.'

Meanwhile, back in Hubcap, Mr Big was standing outside the workshop, whistling and calling. He rustled a packet of Doggy Bites.

'Clutch! Here boy. Where is that blasted dog?'

He heard a clinking sound and out of the darkness came

Clutch, looking extremely groggy. He was dragging his chain which was still attached to the big iron beam. He dropped down at Mr Big's wheels, exhausted.

'Where's the puppy, Clutch? Did you eat him all up like a good boy? Did you?' Mr Big paused, looked at the chain and beam, then said in a very different voice, 'You didn't let him get away again, did you?'

Mr Big extended his antenna. Clutch cringed and crawled away on his belly, whimpering. But all of a sudden he stopped and began to sniff the ground. He got up and sniffed some more, circling round and round until he reached the bushes where Sparky had been hiding. Growling, he followed the trail to the edge of the garage forecourt, looked out into the desert and started barking like crazy.

'What is it?' said Mr Big. 'He's gone? Where? Out into the desert to get help? How can you possibly know that? What are you, Lassie or something?'

Clutch whined desperately. Mr Big undid the chain.

'All right. If that's where he is, go get him!'

Clutch bolted off in a cloud of dust. Mr Big shouted after him as he went.

'And don't come back until you find him!'

First light was dawning as Sparky came to the billabong where Rex had met the RottWheelers. He sniffed around, puzzled by all the criss-crossing paths, but eventually picked up Rex's scent.

'Rex! Where are you?'

His voice echoed amongst the rocks but there was no answer.

He went down to the water's edge. A couple of TruckRoos hopped lazily around to the far side of the pool. As Sparky drank, the TruckRoo reflections shimmered amongst the spreading ripples, then vanished. A moment later they were replaced by another larger reflection. Sparky looked up. Clutch stared back at him across the water.

Sparky leapt backwards with a yell. He spun around in midair and hit the ground running. Clutch launched himself into the waterhole and surged forward, sending a huge wave across the pond. He hauled himself out and set off howling after his prey.

Sparky was out of luck. There was nowhere to hide.

No, wait – in the distance was a rocky outcrop. He couldn't tell how far. He fled towards it . . .

In the inner circle of the rocky outcrop a big meeting of DesertDogs was under way. The whole tribe was there, thirty or more. The one-eyed leader snarled and growled in the snarly growly language of the DesertDogs.

Suddenly the sound of a high-revving engine, accompanied

by a long, terrified yell, broke into his speech, and Sparky hurtled into the clearing. He skidded to a halt right in the middle of the DesertDogs and looked around in utter confusion. They stared back, equally surprised. A second later, Clutch burst into the clearing and slammed into the one-eyed leader, bowling him over. In an instant the DesertDogs were all over him – a biting, scratching, howling ball of teeth, claws and metal. Dog hair and car parts began flying everywhere.

Sparky watched for a moment, then realised no-one was paying any attention to him at all. He edged away, backwards, until he was outside the ring of rocks.

Then he turn and bolted.

Up at Farmer Howell's place, Throttle and Brake were sniffing around, looking for something big to carry the fuel in, as Mr Big had instructed. The stump by the outhouse was still smoking. Throttle wrinkled her nose.

'This place stinks.'

Brake sniffed and shrugged. It smelt all right to him. Suddenly, Throttle stopped and looked out across the paddock. She tapped Brake with the spanner.

'Bingo.'

In the middle distance lay the rusty old tanker hulk that Sparky had stood on to watch the Mongrels sheep-leaping. The

TRUCK**DOGS**

NAME: Norman J. Snitt (Alias: MR BIG)

BREED/MAKE: Chihuahua/BMW Isetta

COLOUR: Light blue/grey

IDENTIFYING MARKS: Permanent snarl, wonky eyes

TEMPERAMENT: Horrid

WARNING
DANGEROUS DOG
DO NOT APPROACH
CALL AUTHORITIES ON SIGHTING
1800BADDOG

FILE INFO:

Leader of RottWheeler Gang. Numerous convictions for theft. Wanted for questioning in regard to recent fuel-scams in Combustion City and neighbouring towns. Seriously unpleasant character. No redeeming feature whatsoever. Probable small-dog inferiority syndrome.

SPECIFICATIONS:

Engine: 1-cylinder, 298cc

Power Output: 13hp

Fuel Requirements: Yours

Maintenance: On demand

flock of TruckSheep were grazing nearby. Throttle noticed one with a set of large curved horns. She frowned.

'Hmmm. We'll have to deal with that big one first. Shouldn't be a problem . . .'

Three minutes later, Throttle and Brake were flying through the air. They came down in the dam with two huge splashes. The TruckRam snorted in satisfaction as they dragged themselves out on the far side.

Throttle shook herself dry, her suspension squeaking as she wriggled her hindquarters.

'Okay,' she said through clenched teeth. 'Plan B.'

Brake shook his head to get the water out of his wing mirrors and squirted a stream of muddy water from his grille. A TruckYabby popped out and clamped onto Throttle's snout.

'Yaaaah!'

Not long after, the TruckRam was back grazing with the TruckSheep when Brake's head appeared from behind a hedge in the next paddock. He went cross-eyed and poked out his tongue. The TruckRam snorted and charged towards him, head down. Suddenly a gate swung shut in front of it. The TruckRam slammed into the gate, entangling its horns in the steel bars of the gate. It struggled furiously to free itself but was caught fast.

Throttle emerged from her hiding place and looked at the TruckRam.

'That should do it. Stupid sheep. Let's get to work.'

They soon had the tanker fastened to Brake's tow bar and were heading back. The big truck sweated and puffed as he hauled the heavy load out onto the road.

'Doing a great job there, Brake,' said Throttle.

Brake just grunted.

The TruckRam was still struggling to disentangle itself from the gate. After they had gone it had one more go at freeing itself, and suddenly the whole gate came off its hinges. The TruckRam tugged again, twisting from side to side, and the lock sheared off, leaving the beast free but with the gate still firmly attached to its head. It looked around with a surprised look as if wondering what to do next, then trotted out onto the road and headed off.

Inside the fuel shed, Mayor Plugg and the Dogsbodys were in a huddle, talking urgently.

'So we're all agreed then,' Mrs Plugg was saying. 'We can't just sit here and wait any longer.' She looked around. 'How're you doing, Mr Howell?'

Farmer Howell was in the corner, looking as if he was about to explode. He gave a little shake of his head.

'Just hold on as long as you can,' said the Mayor.

'What are we going to do?' asked a worried Mrs Dogsbody.

Mayor Plugg held up the screwdriver that she had scooped up in the workshop.

'I'm going to try a little trick my son showed me.'

A little later, as the RottWheeler guards snored, one on each side of the fuel shed, there was a slight bump, a pause, and the shed slowly began to rise up into the air. As it lifted up off its foundations, Mayor Plugg's nose stuck out.

'They're asleep,' she whispered. 'All right, Mrs Dogsbody, lift . . .'

The fuel shed rose up into the air, teetering a little as Mrs Dogsbody's scissor-lift reached its full height. Mayor Plugg, Farmer Howell and Mr Dogsbody crept out from under it. Farmer Howell hurried off.

'At least a hundred metres if you can, please, Mr Howell,' Mayor Plugg called after him in a whisper.

Mr Dogsbody turned back to the shed and reached out with his mobile-crane hook, holding it while Mrs Dogsbody lowered her scissor-lift and joined them outside. Then, carefully, he placed the shed back on its foundations just as a muffled explosion came from the direction of Farmer Howell. It had been a close thing. The four escapees hurriedly crept away.

The RottWheelers stirred, woke and looked around at the

shed. They saw that the door was still bolted. All was well.

Mr Big rolled up.

'What was that bang?'

The RottWheelers shrugged. Mr Big looked at the fuel shed suspiciously. Had it moved a bit to the left?

'Check the shed.'

But just then Throttle arrived. 'We found it, Boss – the perfect thing! One fuel tanker as requested.'

Behind her came Brake, labouring under the weight of the tanker hulk. He was exhausted.

Mr Big practically skipped with delight. 'Excellent! Let us begin!'

He headed off towards the petrol station, Throttle and Brake following.

'It's good to see the boss so happy,' remarked Throttle.

Brake just grunted.

After they had gone, the silhouette of a TruckRam with a gate stuck on top of its head trotted past in the distance, framed against the early morning sky.

Bullworth, Zoe, Prudence and Digger were sitting around a very smoky campfire surrounded by piles of junk. Up above in the desert it was already fully light and beginning to grow hot but the valley was in shadow and still wreathed in the chill of the night.

Digger threw another tyre onto the fire. Prudence coughed as the smoke billowed out.

'Well, that's the last of Cousin Edward,' said Digger. 'He always was a heavy smoker.'

'Ha, ha,' said Prudence.

Zoe looked around the junk piles. 'Where do you reckon Rex and Herc have got to? They've been gone ages.'

Just then, they heard a scrabbling sound above them. A stealthy figure was silhouetted against the light on the ridge above them. It began to make its way down the steep cliff.

'It's a DesertDog!' said Zoe in a frightened whisper. Prudence's hair stood up all the way along her back. Bullworth backed away, eyes bulging. The figure was halfway down the slope when it stumbled and fell, sprawling in a heap at the foot of the stunned TruckDogs.

'Oof!' said Sparky.

'Sparky! What are you doing here?' said Digger.

'And why were you trying to scare us?' added Zoe indignantly.

'I wasn't. Sorry. Ow!' He got up painfully. 'That hurt.'

'I'm not surprised. That was quite an entrance,' said Prudence. 'So, what brings you all the way out here, may I ask?'

'It's Mum – they've got her prisoner – and they're stealing all the fuel – and I got away – and I was looking for Rex – and –'

'Whoa there, slow down. Who's got your Mum prisoner?'

'Mr Big.'

'Mr Who?'

'No, Mr Big. He's a thief. And he's stealing the town's fuel, and Mum has been locked up, and Farmer Howell, too. And —'

Suddenly a large rock came whistling out of the darkness. It thudded into the side of the cliff. A moment later a second rock slammed into Bullworth, breaking into several pieces and knocking the big dozer right over onto his roof.

'Yeeeow!' cried Bullworth.

The others looked around in alarm.

'Sorry, Bullworth!' came Hercules' voice. 'But I told you before that if I meant to hit you, you'd be on your roof!'

The others gawped as Hercules rolled into sight. Two long iron beams ran along either side of his body, attached to his tray by large pivots. A pair of big metal baskets had been bolted onto the ends. The beams were linked to two hydraulic pistons which were in turn hooked up to a large compressor.

'Dual air-powered catapults,' he explained in answer to their baffled expressions.

He jiggled his rear suspension, flipping a couple of rocks out of his tray, one into each basket, then took aim at a tall crane that was sticking up out of the junk piles and fired. The first rock hit the crane, spinning it round and sending the dangling hook swinging on its cable. The second rock hit the hook which wrapped itself tightly around the crane. Then the whole thing collapsed.

The onlookers whistled appreciatively.

'Hey, could someone help me up?' called Bullworth. He wiggled his caterpillar tracks helplessly, like a turtle on its back, but the others were too engrossed in Hercules' new toy.

Prudence examined the contraption. 'Where'd you find this thing anyway?'

'Rex made it.'

'Rex built this?' said Prudence.

'Awesome!' exclaimed Digger. 'Why?'

Rex chugged up behind Hercules. He looked at Sparky. 'It seems the answer to that has just arrived.'

'Rex!' cried Sparky joyously.

'Things beginning to hot up back in town, eh?'

Sparky nodded.

Behind them, Bullworth was still struggling. 'Hey, guys – help me up!'

'What's going on?' asked Hercules, noticing Sparky for the first time. 'What are you doing here?'

Sparky told his story again, more slowly this time. When he finished they sat for a moment in silence.

Then Rex spoke. 'All right, listen to me, all of you. Here comes the speech. In every machine there are many parts, each with its own purpose. Even the smallest cog in the biggest machine has a vital job to do. It is part of the whole. Without it the machine does not work as it should. You youngsters have energy to burn. It's what got you in trouble back in Hubcap. It's also your greatest strength. Well, now the time has come to put all that young energy to good use. Your home is in peril. And you have a job to do.'

Digger looked puzzled. 'Maybe I'm missing something but didn't those old fleabags just run us out of town?'

'We're a public nuisance,' said Bullworth.

'Rude, impudent vandals, as I recall,' said Prudence.

Sparky looked at Rex in despair. But Rex's eyes were unreadable. He remained silent.

'They ran us out of town all right,' said Hercules. 'They're narrow-minded, selfish, intolerant, gutless – and old.' He paused. 'Which is why they need us. Hubcap is our town too. They may be living in the past – but we are the future!'

'Yay!' cried Zoe.

'Woo hoo!' hooted Digger.

Rex smiled.

'Yeah, great,' said Bullworth. 'And I'm still upside down. Come on, guys!'

Hercules turned to Sparky. 'How much time do we have?'

'Not much. They're going to take all the fuel – every drop, they said – then blow up the fuel shed. We've got to save Mum!'

'All the fuel?' said Rex. ' They'll have to find something to carry it in . . . and pumping it out will take time . . .' He thought for a moment. 'We've got maybe twenty-four hours. Come on, we have to prepare ourselves.'

'Does that mean I get a catapult, too?' asked Digger hopefully.

TRUCKDOGS

NAME: THROTTLE

BREED/MAKE: Greyhound/Drag Car

COLOUR: Red with broad yellow stripe

IDENTIFYING MARKS: Large mole on RHS front panel, fake ruby-studded collar

TEMPERAMENT: Arrogant, vicious and immoral (but otherwise she's really delightful)

FILE INFO:

Member of RottWheeler Gang. Second in command to Mr Big (File No 00228309). Wanted for questioning in regard to recent fuel-scams in Combustion City and neighbouring towns. Numerous convictions for speeding.

SPECIFICATIONS:

Engine: Single rear-mount Aerospace ramjet

Power Output: Enormous

Fuel Requirements: Designed for high-grade aviation fuel but modified to run on premium unleaded instead

Maintenance: General overhaul every Wednesday afternoon

'No. The catapult is for Hercules. It is an extension of his natural strengths. I made it for him alone.'

'So what do we get?' asked Prudence.

'Well,' said Rex, 'let's see what you're good at.'

They headed off, leaving Bullworth still upside down.

The Pack gathered around Rex in an open space between the junk piles.

'We'll start with rocks,' said Rex. Digger whooped enthusiastically and bounded off to find some big ones.

Zoe found a small boulder nearby but try as she might she couldn't flip it up at all. The rough edges of the rock were giving her blisters on her tyre walls. Prudence had no more success, though she eventually managed to roll a small round one down a slope with her snout, hitting a still-upside-down Bullworth on the nose.

'Sorry, Bullworth. What are you doing lying down on the job?'

'Yeah, c'mon, Bullyboy. We've got work to do,' added Hercules.

'Very funny.'

Sparky was about to have a go at the rock when they heard Digger's voice. 'Watch this!' he called, struggling up to them with a huge boulder loaded into his back hoe. 'Hold still, Bullworth.'

'Don't you dare!'

But before Digger could fire, he over-balanced backwards

and found himself staring skyward with his front wheels in the air.

With a huge effort Bullworth at last managed to roll himself right-way up.

'Right, it's payback time!' He scooped up Prudence's rock in his mouth, crunched it into gravel and sprayed it out like a scatter gun.

'Yeow!' cried Digger, scrambling back to his wheels. The others squealed and ran for cover. Bullworth charged off after them.

After the others had gone, Sparky tried to move Digger's boulder with his snout.

Not a chance.

Digger was determined to get the rock-throwing right. After all, he figured, he already had a built-in catapult in his back hoe. Zoe watched with amusement as he shunted another huge boulder into his hoe and struggled to lift it.

'C'mon, Digger, put some effort into it.'

Digger gritted his teeth and strained mightily. Suddenly the whole back-hoe arm came off, sending him tumbling forwards.

'Ouch – that must have hurt,' winced Zoe. 'Hey, Herc, can you come here a moment? Digger seems to have been rendered armless.'

In response to the pathetic joke, Digger shoved her into the side of a nearby water tank. Dirty water sloshed out all over her just as Hercules came up.

'Yeeeee! I *hate* that!' she cried. 'I just *hate* it!'

Hercules laughed. Zoe glared at him. Then she looked up at the tank with a cunning smile.

Rex was busy, meanwhile, showing Bullworth how to move large objects by a combination of leverage, body placement and sheer force of will. Thin and weedy though he was, the old tractor put his wheel to a huge old pumping engine and shifted it backwards a good two metres.

'Remember, you have to *want* to move it. Decide you are going to do it – then do it.'

Bullworth nodded, took a couple of deep breaths and put his head down. He strained until he was blue in the face and his teeth hurt. The pumping engine didn't budge an inch.

'Ow. My eef urt,' said Bullworth, feeling around his mouth.

'Hmmm' said Rex. 'Looks like some dental work is in order. I'll get back to you.'

Zoe trundled by with a length of garden hose and some baling wire between her teeth. She carried it to the water tank and added it to her stash, which already included a compressor and a big brass nozzle from an old fire engine. Her plan was coming together.

Later in the day, Hercules was practising with his catapult when suddenly a stream of freezing water hit him in the face.

'Bleargh! Hey, what the . . .' He spun round to find Zoe

looking innocently at the sky, whistling. Mounted on her roof was the water tank and compressor. A length of garden hose ran from her mixer, which was full of cold water, to the compressor. Another length was looped around a garden rake at the end of which was tied the brass fire-engine nozzle.

He frowned at her sternly. 'Now, listen here . . .'

But she just pointed the nozzle at him and fired another burst of water, then fled, laughing, with the big ore truck in hot pursuit.

On the other side of the junkyard Rex stood back and admired his handiwork. He had fitted Bullworth with a reinforced dozer front bucket made from the old plough and a huge truck gearbox. He adjusted it, checking that the circular plough blades spun freely, and pronounced it finished. It looked very fearsome indeed.

'All right, now you have no excuse. You can do it – so do it!'

Bullworth lowered his head, lined himself up with the huge pumping engine and pushed. He shunted it right across the junkyard, and crunched into the cliffs on the far side. An avalanche of rocks rained down, burying him up to his roof. His exhaust stack, which was poking up out of the rocks, belched smoke as he revved his engine. He engaged his gear-box, spun the plough shares like a massive blender, and the rock pile was rapidly ground down into gravel. Bullworth emerged, one happy and proud dozer.

'I'm unstoppable!' he cried.

'Yes,' laughed Rex. 'I believe you are.'

Darkness fell and still the TruckDogs worked. Rex moved between them offering advice and encouragement.

Prudence was searching through the junk looking for inspiration when she came across a firebox belonging to an old traction engine. She filled it with coals from the camp fire and blew through it from behind. A cloud of black smoke erupted from it, making Digger cough and choke just as he was trying yet again to get a rock into the air.

The rock came down on his cab, squashing it flat.

Digger held his breath and blew through his gaskets, popping his cab back into shape. He found Rex watching and shaking his head. 'I think we're barking up the wrong tree here, Digger. A rock-thrower you most definitely are not. Can you dig?'

'Can I dig? Hey, I'm a labrador!'

Rex nodded towards an enormous auger lying amidst the junk – a giant drill bit used to dig post holes. 'You, my friend, are going to dig like no other labrador in history!'

Dawn was not far off as Rex finished attaching the auger to Digger's back hoe, tightening the bolts with his teeth.

'You could do with a spanner,' remarked Digger.

'I've got a spanner,' replied Rex. He paused. 'I just don't have it with me right now.'

The auger was linked to Digger's main drive shaft with a series of belts and pulleys. Digger held it poised over his head like a scorpion's tail.

'This is great!' he said excitedly. 'I've gotta dig something!'

He lifted the auger high above his head and quickly gouged a deep hole in the cliff face. Rex nodded, satisfied. Digger pointed the drill downwards and within moments had dug a two-metre-deep hole in the rocky ground.

'Awesome!' He put the drill into reverse and revved, but the bit jammed, spinning him around in circles instead. Rex shook his head – there was more work to do yet.

Sparky had been watching. Digging holes was surely some-thing all TruckDogs could do. He waited until they had gone off to make some improvements to the auger, then set to work. But when Rex and Digger passed by a little later, the hole he had made was only a tenth of Digger's effort and he was exhausted.

Digger looked rather smugly at Sparky's hole in the dirt but before he could comment there was a deafening roar from behind him. Digger leapt in fright and spun around to find himself enveloped in a huge cloud of acrid smoke. He coughed and gasped. A vast armour-plated dragon with horns and a visor like a knight's helmet appeared out of the cloud, snorting and smoking. The long body was lined with steel plates, like scales topped with jagged points all the way down the spine. The firebox, slung in front of the grille, was filled with coals and smouldering tyres.

The dragon raised its visor. 'So, what do you think?'

Digger circled Prudence's outfit and nodded appreciatively. 'Smokin'!'

The two went off together to plan tactics, leaving a rather forlorn-looking Sparky behind.

'Why so glum?' asked Rex. 'Seems you've lost all your bounce.'

'It's nothing.' Sparky scuffed his wheels in the dust. 'It's just that I'm not really good at *anything*.'

Rex considered this for a moment, then seemed to come to a decision. 'Yep, that's definitely the problem. You've lost your bounce. Come with me.'

He led Sparky to another part of the junkyard, beyond the steel girders and wrecked vehicles.

'I bet we can find your bounce somewhere here.'

Sparky gazed up at a mountain of coiled springs, shock absorbers and suspension struts of every size and shape. His tail began to wag.

The sun was rising over the rim of the world, casting a golden glow over the desert, when at last the Mongrel Pack were all gathered together in their armour – Proud Hercules with his catapults, Bullworth with his plough blades, Zoe with her water cannon, Digger with his auger and Prudence in her dragon suit.

'Where's Sparky?' asked Digger.

'Here!' cried Sparky, bounding in. He was wearing a safety helmet with a flashing light and a new power-spring suspension system featuring four massive hydraulic shock absorbers.

'Watch this!' He crouched down, then leapt straight up – six metres clear of the ground.

'Whoa!' he cried as he struggled to maintain control, bouncing several times before landing dangerously close to Bullworth's new rotor blades.

'Impressive ground clearance,' said Digger.

'Matched by enviable ride and handling,' said Prudence.

'And ready for anything!' cried Sparky.

Suddenly a terrible howling broke out. They looked around in alarm as twenty or more DesertDogs swarmed down the slopes above them and over the piles of junk. The one-eyed leader snarled in puzzlement at the TruckDogs' strange outfits. But then he barked an order and the DesertDogs attacked.

The Mongrel Pack's new accessories gave them a definite advantage over their attackers. The DesertDogs yelped and howled as they fended off hurtling boulders, jets of water, spinning ploughshares, razor-sharp augers and clouds of blinding smoke. But they were ferocious fighters and greater in number. They swarmed over the junk towards their foe.

Rex was especially targeted. Sparky saw him surrounded by ten or more DesertDogs. He set his new suspension to maximum clearance and sprang to his aid, but couldn't control the

TRUCK**DOGS**

NAME: BRAKE

BREED/MAKE: Mastiff/Monster Truck
COLOUR: Blue
IDENTIFYING MARKS: Numerous self-inflicted tattoos and piercings
TEMPERAMENT: Thick as a ten-tonne-truck tyre

FILE INFO:
Senior member of RottWheeler Gang (Chief Navigator).
Wanted in relation to 376 outstanding parking tickets.

SPECIFICATIONS:
Engine: Twin V12 turbos
Power Output: 500kW at 5000 rpm
Fuel Requirements: 10 litres per 100 metres
Maintenance: Duh?

new springs and went bouncing wildly all over the place. On a couple of bounces he connected with a DesertDog, but just as often landed on one of his fellow TruckDogs (with a cry of 'sorry!'). At one point he scored a direct hit on the one-eyed leader, coming down hard on his tailpipe. The Dog spun around yelping in pain and fury but couldn't work out where the attack had come from as Sparky had already bounced off again over the junk piles.

The battle raged back and forth, but at last the DesertDogs were beaten. They retreated, howling, scrabbling back up the cliffs into the night. The Mongrel Pack cheered in victory.

Hercules flexed his catapults. 'Hey, Rex, these things are not bad – not bad at all!' He looked around. 'Rex?'

The old tractor was nowhere in sight.

'Rex? Where are you?' called Sparky. A familiar hubcap lay in the dirt. A little further on was Rex's funnel. Sparky was filled with a sudden dread.

They searched urgently, calling out Rex's name, until at last they found him lying amongst the junk. His old body blended in with the battered old machinery so well he was almost invisible. Around him lay the wrecks of several DesertDogs. He was badly damaged, a deep rent in one wheel arch, a gaping hole at his funnel outlet. The left rear wheel had been ripped off at the axle and was nowhere in sight. Engine oil seeped from a puncture in his sump.

The Mongrels gathered round him anxiously.

'Rex! Say something,' cried Sparky. 'Anything!'

'Woof,' said Rex weakly.

'Okay, that'll do,' said Prudence. 'At least he's alive.'

Hercules frowned. 'We need to get him to a mechanic. Come on, guys. Help me lift him.'

But Rex shook his head. 'There's no time. You have to get back to Hubcap. 'Besides,' he managed a smile, lifting himself with some effort up on one axle. 'I'm a mechanic. It'll just take me . . . a little time . . . to fix myself up.'

'We can't just leave you here,' protested Sparky. 'What if the DesertDogs come back?'

'I doubt they will. But if they do I'll be ready for them.' He looked at the junk lying around him. 'I've plenty of good material to work with.'

Sparky hesitated, unwilling to leave his friend, but Hercules nodded. 'Rex is right. We have to go. Hubcap needs us.' He turned to Sparky. 'And we need you with us, partner.'

Sparky looked at Hercules, then the other TruckDogs. 'You mean . . . I'm a member of the Mongrel Pack?'

'Sure,' smiled Prudence. 'Unless you'd rather join the Cosmic Tractors?'

Sparky beamed. 'Oh, boy! I always wanted to be one of you guys!' He looked back at Rex in concern.

'I'm all right,' said the old tractor reassuringly. 'Your town needs you. Go.'

The Mongrels looked at each other, a team, bonded by their past, their present and their future. Then they revved their engines, crunched themselves into gear and roared off into the sunrise.

BITE THREE

Meanwhile, back in Hubcap, things were looking grim. Up at the garage the fuel-pumping operation was well underway. One of the Rott-Wheelers monitored the flow at a valve connected to the underground fuel-storage tank. Another held the hose steady, pouring the fuel into the rusty old tanker. Brake was still attached to the tanker. He was sweating heavily.

Throttle was overseeing operations, practising spinning the big silver spanner with one wheel. She fumbled and it fell to the ground.

'Stupid spanner – out of balance,' she muttered.

The townsfolk were all staying safely indoors, but on the far side of the workshop, Mayor Plugg, Farmer Howell and the Dogsbodys were watching, their bonnets poking out from between a row of low shrubs. An engine approaching from further up the street made them pull back quickly.

It was Mr Big.

The little chihuahua rolled up and surveyed the scene,

nodding in satisfaction. At that moment there was a gurgling sound and the RottWheeler monitoring the valve called out that the tank was empty. The other RottWheeler held the hose up, dripping.

Throttle turned to Mr Big. 'That's it, Boss.'

Watching from their hiding place, Mayor Plugg whispered hopefully to the others. 'They don't know about tank two!'

Out on the forecourt, Mr Big turned to Mr Barker, who was hovering nearby. 'Open up tank two.'

Mr Barker gulped. 'Er, we only have one tank,' he said, unconvincingly.

'Listen, Delivery Boy, I do a lot of this kind of thing. I know you have a second tank. Now open it up or we'll drain you dry as well.'

Mr Barker pushed aside an engine-oil display rack, revealing the access hatch to the town's emergency fuel-storage tank.

'I'll kill him,' hissed Mrs Dogsbody.

'Not if I get to him first,' said Farmer Howell.

'Without fuel this town is as good as dead,' said Mayor Plugg. 'We have to make a stand. Let's go and spread the word.' She and the others headed off.

'That's better,' said Mr Big as the two RottWheelers slid the access hatch off. He turned and snarled at Mr Barker. 'Now get out of my sight.'

Mr Barker skulked off. The RottWheelers connected the

TRUCKDOGS

NAME: CLUTCH

BREED/MAKE: Bull Terrier/Heavy Haulage Hybrid
COLOUR: Albino
IDENTIFYING MARKS: Leather restraining muzzle, wild red eyes
TEMPERAMENT: Totally insane

WARNING
DO NOT APPROACH
CALL AUTHORITIES ON SIGHTING
1800BADDOG

FILE INFO:
Mr Big's 'pet', used for tracking work and Hunter/Killer missions. Very Dangerous.

SPECIFICATIONS:
Engine: Marine diesel/steam-engine composite
Power Output: 30 knots into the breeze
Fuel Requirements: Diesel and coal in equal parts
Maintenance: None to date

hose to the second tank and started pumping again. The tanker creaked under the weight.

'Heavy. Getting . . . heavy,' groaned Brake.

'Don't be such a wus,' said Throttle, then to the RottWheelers, 'Check the level.'

The tanker was three-quarters full. Throttle looked questioningly at Mr Big.

'I want all of it,' he growled. 'Every last drop. Keep filling.'

'You got it, Boss.' Throttle went to spin the spanner again but thought better of it.

Mayor Plugg, Farmer Howell and the Dogsbodys moved quietly and quickly from house to house, keeping out of sight, taking the backstreets, spreading the word amongst the townsfolk.

Farmer Howell found Mr Scratchly outside his shop.

'We're going to stand and fight,' he said conspiratorially. 'Meet at the statue in one hour.'

'Eh? What's that?'

Farmer Howell spoke a little louder. 'We're going to make a stand. The statue. One hour.'

Mr Barker wandered by on the other side of the street. He stopped and watched.

'Spweak up, will you?' Mr Scratchly fiddled with his hearing aid. 'Stop mumbwing!'

'I said meet at the statue, you deaf coot!' shouted Farmer

Howell. 'They're stealing all our fuel! We've got to stop them!'

'All wight, there's no need to showt,' said Mr Scratchly crossly and went back into his shop. Farmer Howell rolled his eyes and motored off. Across the street, Mr Barker thought a moment, then, with a shifty look, turned and headed back towards the petrol station.

A moment later the TruckRam trotted by, the gate still firmly entangled in its horns.

The townsfolk gathered at the remains of the statue in the Hubcap Memorial Park. Mayor Plugg stood by the big tree flanked by Farmer Howell and Mr and Mrs Dogsbody and addressed the crowd.

'All right, everyone. If I can have your attention please. It's come down to this: either we make a stand or we lose our fuel – and if we lose our fuel, our town cannot survive. We have no option. We have to fight.'

A murmur ran through the crowd.

Edna Fleasome tut-tutted. 'Fight? For ourselves? We should have police or an army or something to fight for us. Really, this town is going to the dogs.'

'Going to the dogs,' echoed Ida.

'It's going to its grave if we don't do something,' said Mrs Dogsbody sharply. 'Stop whining.'

'Well!' said Edna in her most affronted voice.

'Well!' said Ida.

'And stop repeating everything she says! Why don't you think for yourself?'

Edna and Ida were most indignant. But they shut up.

'Listen, everyone, please,' said Mayor Plugg. 'We must work together. United we stand –'

'And divided you fall,' came Mr Big's voice.

Everyone spun around. To their horror they found the park surrounded by a snarling ring of RottWheelers. Mr Big rolled forward.

'Was that what you were going to say, Mayor Plugg? Because divided you most certainly are.'

Mayor Plugg looked past Mr Big and saw Mr Barker standing behind him.

'Thank you, Mr Barker, for your most useful information. Paid for in full with one tank of premium unleaded, as agreed, and a year's supply of brake fluid. I trust you are satisfied?'

Mr Barker did not reply.

Mayor Plugg looked at him and shook her head. 'Why, Mr Barker?'

Mr Barker's eye twitched. He answered angrily, defensively. 'We all need fuel, you know. This town is finished without it.' He jerked his head towards the desert. 'It's a long way to the next pump.'

Mrs Plugg nodded slowly. 'It is indeed, Mr Barker. It is indeed.' Her voice became hard. 'Drive safely, won't you?'

The townsfolk glared at Mr Barker in silence. He looked around, then averted his eyes and drove off. Mr Big returned his attention to Mayor Plugg.

'Now, where were we? Oh, yes . . .' He paused. 'This is a little embarrassing, actually. I would normally ask Clutch to tear you to pieces at this point, but he has been unavoidably delayed – doing exactly that to your son Sparky, I believe.'

He paused for a reaction from Mrs Plugg but her face remained fixed, her expression unreadable. Mr Big continued with a shrug. 'So anyway, I have asked the rest of the gang to fill in for Clutch. So now we're going to tear the whole town apart!'

The RottWheelers bared their teeth and began to move in on their prey. Mayor Plugg, Farmer Howell and the Dogsbodys prepared themselves.

'Stay calm,' called Mayor Plugg to the frightened townsfolk. 'Don't run or they will chase you.'

Suddenly the noise of other engines was heard over the sound of the RottWheelers, a huge roaring that seemed to be everywhere, echoing off the buildings, filling the air. Mr Big looked around in puzzlement, unable to work out where it was coming from.

Then suddenly it stopped.

Into the silence came a voice, speaking through a megaphone.

'Attention, Mr Big and accomplices. You are surrounded. Switch your engines off, put your gearboxes in neutral and turn your wheels to the kerb.'

Mr Big whirled around but could not find the source of the voice.

It spoke again, this time without the megaphone. 'Up here, shorty.'

Mr Big looked up to find Sparky standing atop the Town Hall. 'You!'

'Sparky! You're alive!' cried Mayor Plugg.

'Hi, Mum.' He motioned towards Mr Big. 'That little yap dog down there causing a problem?'

Mayor Plugg looked at Mr Big and his thugs. 'Well, kind of . . .'

'Don't worry. We've got everything under control.' He raised the megaphone again and addressed the RottWheelers. 'You have made a big mistake taking on this town. Drive away now and no-one gets hurt.'

Throttle sneered. 'Hah! Says you and what army?'

'This one,' came a voice. There was a mighty revving of an engine. Hercules drove into view and everyone looked with amazement at his spectacular refit.

Throttle scoffed. 'That's no army. It's just a kid with a catapult.'

Hercules' twin compressors burst into life, catapulting a pair of enormous boulders into the air. They came crashing down, one just in front of Throttle's nose, one just behind her tailpipe. She was clearly rattled but managed another sneer.

'Missed.'

'If I'd meant to miss –' began Hercules.

'. . . you'd be on your roof,' finished Bullworth, rumbling into view from the opposite direction. The crowd gasped at the sight of his spectacular ploughshare dozer blade.

'What is this?' demanded Mr Big. 'A freak show? Where's the next clown going to pop out from?'

As if in answer, a deep rumbling was heard. The ground shook like an earthquake and a huge drill burst up directly under one of the RottWheelers, sending dirt flying everywhere. The unfortunate vehicle squealed in surprise. When the townsfolk looked again, a dirt-encrusted monster was clambering out of a gaping hole in the ground. Even Mr Big's eyes bulged. The creature shook itself off, revealing itself to be Digger. He nodded to the watching crowd.

'G'day, folks. How's it going?'

'This is ridiculous,' snapped Mr Big. 'Who are you? Where did you come from?'

Sparky replied from the rooftop. 'Round here actually. We're just little cogs in a big machine. But today we plan to make a difference.'

Prudence appeared in her armour. Mr Big rolled his eyes. 'Oh, great. And what are you supposed to be?'

'Guess.'

Prudence roared through her firebox, singeing Mr Big's whiskers to stubble and covering him in a thick coat of smoke and ash. He blinked stupidly and coughed out a puff of ash.

'A dragon?' he said weakly. He sneezed violently. An instant later a huge burst of water hit him in the face.

'Ergch!'

Zoe rolled up with her water cannon dripping. 'Getting a little hot under the collar? There you go, little fella. Bath time.'

Mr Big shook himself, looking very much like a drowned TruckRat. The RottWheelers stood looking at him, grilles gaping.

'Don't just stand there gawping, you idiots,' Mr Big screeched. 'Get them!'

'Attack!' yelled Throttle, who was still pinned by the two boulders. As if released from a trance, the RottWheelers surged forward and the battle was joined.

The Mongrel Pack were ready and waiting. Zoe turned as a RottWheeler charged at her, snarling. He got her water cannon full in the face and backed off, choking and gagging. Another RottWheeler launched himself at Digger's flank. Digger spun his back hoe around and drilled into the RottWheeler's wind-screen, scratching across it with an ear-splitting *skritchchchch*. The RottWheeler bolted, squealing.

Bullworth scooped up a rock in his huge jaws, chomped

it into gravel and, with his ploughshare blades spinning, pumped it out. The stones hit the spinning ploughshares as he adjusted the blade angle, sending stinging shrapnel ricocheting this way and that. The RottWheelers yelped and ducked.

Sparky leapt from the Town Hall roof, howling like a DesertDog. 'Howoowoooowooooo!'

He landed full on a RottWheeler, crushing the cab flat, and bounced off again, high into the air, out of control. 'Whoaaaa!'

Throttle, meanwhile, was struggling to extricate herself from between the boulders, but she was stuck fast. She smashed at them with Rex's spanner, with no result except to mark the otherwise pristine tool.

Mayor Plugg rallied the townsfolk, who had been watching open-mouthed. 'Come on, everyone! This is our town. Let's fight for it!'

The townsfolk erupted in a battle-cry, howling and revving, and surged forward to join the Mongrel Pack. Even Edna and Ida joined in.

'Let's bag ourselves some RottWheeler,' cried Ida. Edna looked at her sister in shock.

At that moment a huge, slavering RottWheeler bore down on them. It snapped at Edna viciously. She swung the handbag that hung on her wing mirror and whacked the TruckDog sharply on the nose.

'How dare you, you disgusting creature,' she scolded.

TRUCK DOGS

NAME: FARMER HOWELL
BREED/MAKE: Red Heeler/Ford 50 Pick-up
COLOUR: Burgundy — or is it claret?
IDENTIFYING MARKS: More of a smell really
TEMPERAMENT: Well-ventilated

FILE INFO:
Age: No-one's willing to ask.
Address: Up at the Farm, but he
don't want no visitors, you hear?

SPECIFICATIONS:
Engine: -cylinder, 5.0 Litre
Fuel Requirements: Continuous
Maintenance: Whenever. Whatever.

COMMENTS
Crusty old fart but decent enough deep, deep down

(Note also: Poultry/Seed Planter TruckChook)

'What would your mother say? You are a disgrace! Now, get out of my sight!'

The RottWheeler backed off, utterly intimidated, as another gang member passed by.

'She's horrible!' he said, glancing at Edna, tears welling. 'She says the most awful things!'

Edna turned to Ida triumphantly. 'There. That'll teach him.'

'You said it, sis! Woo hoo!'

Edna stared at her. Ida shrugged.

Across the park, Mr Scratchly had been pinned against a tree by another RottWheeler. Mr Dogsbody came up behind the thug, lifted him bodily off the ground with his crane and hooked him to a branch by his collar.

'Stay,' he said sternly.

Mrs Dogsbody, meanwhile, found herself confronted by a particularly large and ugly brute. She backed away until she was hard up against the side of the Town Hall. The RottWheeler grinned nastily. She continued to back up the wall until she was vertical, facing the ground, then suddenly shot out her scissor lift like an extendable boxing glove. *Boof!* The RottWheeler was sent reeling.

Mr Big looked around at the confusion. Throttle was still struggling between the boulders.

'Hey, Boss!' she called. 'Help me.'

But the fighting was getting too hot for Mr Big. Ignoring her, he called to some nearby RottWheelers.

'You two, come with me back to the petrol station. Everyone else, help hold them off. We'll, er . . . wait for you down the road.'

He took off in a hurry. Throttle saw him go. With a furious effort she struggled up and clambered over the front boulder. She had almost made it when there was a cry of 'Whoaaaa!' from above and Sparky landed right in front of her, bouncing off again with another cry. Throttle fell backwards onto her roof and found herself stuck upside down between the boulders. She wriggled her wheels in fury.

Bullworth rolled up to her. 'Hey, I know what it's like,' he commiserated. 'You've just got to relax. Think like a turtle.'

'What? Shut up, you overgrown Tonka toy!'

Bullworth shrugged, put his dozer blade to the boulders and pushed them even more tightly together.

'Eeech! You're squashing me!'

'It's what I'm good at.'

Mr Big and the two RottWheelers returned to the petrol station. Brake was there, waiting, still attached to the tanker. 'What's happening, Boss?'

'Where were you when we needed you, you big oaf?' panted Mr Big.

Brake struggled under the weight. 'Too heavy. Can't . . . move.'

'Is all the fuel on board?'

Brake managed to nod.

Mr Big turned to the RottWheelers. 'Okay, get him moving – give him a push.'

The RottWheelers drove up to the back of the tanker and pushed, but he wouldn't budge. Just then, Throttle arrived, having at last managed to free herself. She looked a mess, her paintwork scratched and dented, her rear wheels wobbling on their axle. Mr Big glanced at her, then back at the struggling RottWheelers.

'Come on! Push!'

'No really, I'm fine,' said Throttle sarcastically. 'Thanks for asking.'

'Yeah, whatever. I'm getting out of here.'

'What happened to Clutch?'

'Who knows? Damn dog has disappeared, useless mutt. Never liked him anyway.'

'No,' said Throttle with emphasis, looking behind Mr Big's shoulder. 'I mean, *what happened to Clutch?*'

Mr Big turned to find Clutch standing there, bruised and battered, his collar hanging half off, torn and tattered. The huge beast looked at Mr Big, puzzled, hurt. And for the first time he spoke.

'Master – no – like – Clutch?'

'Oh, there you are,' said Mr Big. Then he looked around and frowned. 'No puppy again? I told you not to come back without him.'

He tapped his antenna but, rather than cringing, Clutch started to move forward, his red albino eyes fixed on Mr Big.

'Master no like Clutch. Cruel master. Bad master!'

'Now, now. That's not what I meant. I meant . . . er . . . Throttle, what did I mean?'

Throttle shrugged. 'Don't ask me.'

Mr Big fumbled for a packet of Doggy Bites but his glove box was empty. He backed away, holding his antenna out in front of him. He stumbled on a tree root, regained his balance and began to slash wildly as Clutch bore down on him.

'Get away from me, you monster!'

Clutch caught the antenna in his mouth, bit off the end and chomped it up. Mr Big wet his wheels, turned and fled. Clutch sprang after him with a roar.

'*Yipe! Yipe! Yipe! Yipe!*' squealed Mr Big.

One of the RottWheelers standing by the tanker looked at Mr Big, then at Throttle. 'Should we, like, save him or something?'

Throttle looked at Brake, 'What do you reckon, Brake?'

Brake grunted. It sounded like no.

The battle between the townsfolk and the rest of the RottWheelers was getting closer. A flying RottWheeler landed at Throttle's wheels with a thud.

Throttle looked at the senseless vehicle in alarm. 'Okay. I say we save the fuel and get out of here. Brake, *get moving!*'

Brake strained mightily. 'Aaaaaargh!'

There was a grinding noise and a loud clunk and he collapsed onto his springs, smoke billowing out of his engine.

'Brake broke,' he groaned.

'Oh, this is just great,' muttered Throttle. She glanced up at the approaching townsfolk. The time had definitely come to be somewhere else.

Mr Big fled into the workshop and slammed the door. He looked around in desperation and scurried under a tarpaulin by the back wall. A moment later Clutch smashed through the door, splintering it into a million pieces. He stopped, looked around and saw the tarpaulin trembling . . .

'Master no like Clutch. Clutch no like Master!'

But as Clutch stood looking down at the quivering lump, Mr Big leapt up and threw the tarpaulin over him. Clutch fell back with a roar, struggling to free himself. He knocked a half-full can of diesel over, soaking the sheet.

Mr Big got out his lighter. He flicked it alight, held it over Clutch and dropped it.

'Oops.'

The tarpaulin erupted into flames. Clutch began to thrash about wildly.

Mr Big hurried to the doorway, poked his nose out to check the coast was clear, and hurried off.

Mr Scratchly scurried down a narrow lane pursued by a huge RottWheeler. He turned a corner and skidded quickly into a hiding spot between two water tanks. A moment later the RottWheeler roared past.

'Now!' he yelled.

A huge jet of flame shot out from the other side of the lane, accompanied by a juicy bang, roasting the passing RottWheeler. It disappeared into the desert, yelping. Farmer Howell emerged, smoking. The two TruckDogs did a high five.

'You're really firing today, Farmer Howell!' said Mr Scratchly.

Farmer Howell winked. 'It's what I'm good at.'

Most of the fighting was still centred around the Memorial Park and further up the main street, but Sparky had bounced across to the petrol station. He was busy flattening out one of the RottWheelers when suddenly he smelt something. He looked up and saw a wisp of smoke rising from behind the garage.

'The workshop's on fire!' he cried.

He bounced once more on the RottWheeler, knocking him out cold. Prudence looked up from over the road as he raced off.

At the workshop door, or what remained of it, Sparky was

greeted by billowing smoke and tongues of fire. He tried to see into the building but the smoke was too thick. Was that whimpering he could hear?

'Hello!' he called. 'Is anyone in there?'

He cocked his head and listened. The sound of whimpering was clearer this time. Gathering himself, he sprang over the flames to the far side.

Clutch was cowering at the back of the workshop. Sparky skidded to a halt.

'Aaagh! YOU!'

He scrabbled round and made to leap back to the doorway. Clutch stared at him, shaking in terror, a pitiable sight.

Sparky paused, confused.

'C'mon,' he said, keeping his distance. 'Just smash your way out! You can do that.' But the monster was immobile, petrified.

By now the fire was making its way along the back wall. Sparky looked through the rising flames towards the doorway – it was now or never.

Clutch whimpered again.

Sparky could not leave him to die. Clutch might be a psychotic monster with a murderous bent, but he was still a living creature. Sparky knew what he had to do.

A ramp along the side wall led up to a mezzanine floor where old timbers and junk were stored. The fire had not reached it yet.

'Listen . . . Clutch. Look at me. We're going up that ramp, okay? Come on.'

He held Clutch's eyes and began backing up the ramp, speaking softly. 'Come on.'

Clutch moved forward slowly. He began to climb up the ramp. An overhead beam collapsed in a shower of sparks. The ramp sagged alarmingly. Clutch froze, terrified.

'It's okay,' Sparky said soothingly. 'We can do this. Come on now.'

Clutch continued to creep forward . . .

Outside, Prudence came up to the warehouse just as a huge cloud of sparks billowed up into the air. She jumped back in alarm.

'Zoe! Fire-engine duty! Zoe, where are you?'

Near the windmill, Zoe was bailed up by a pair of Rott-Wheelers, one in front of her, snarling, the other behind, snapping at her axle.

'Get away from me, you ugly beasts!' she cried and kicked out at them with her rear wheels. She fired her cannon but they were too close, ducking under the water jet.

Down the hill Hercules saw her peril. He scooped up a boulder, took aim and fired.

'Zoe, duck!' he yelled.

Zoe ducked. So did the first RottWheeler. The second one didn't. The boulder slammed into him, shunting him backwards

116

TRUCK**DOGS**

NAME: TRUCKRAM

BREED/MAKE: Merino/VW Kombi
COLOUR: Aqua and cream two-tone
IDENTIFYING MARKS: You mean apart from the enormous horns?
TEMPERAMENT: Very baaaad-tempered

FILE INFO:
Age: unknown — looks Jurassic. Property of Farmer Howell.

SPECIFICATIONS:
Engine: 4-cylinder, air-cooled
Fuel Requirements: Grass, and lots of it
Maintenance: Yearly dip and de-dag if you're brave enough

(Note also: Merino/VW Beetle TruckSheep)

into the windmill, which shuddered on its foundations. The first RottWheeler looked up at the windmill, then back at Hercules just in time for a second boulder to slam into him. Zoe side-stepped nimbly as he was shunted into the other RottWheeler. The windmill buckled and toppled, crashing down on the two RottWheelers in a tangled mess of iron.

Hercules rolled up to Zoe.

'You okay?' he asked in his best screen-hero voice.

'Oh, Herc, you saved me!' Zoe swooned.

He bent over for the kiss he so clearly deserved – and instead got a face full of water as Zoe squirted him and wriggled away.

'No way, you big Alfa Romeo!'

'Bleargh! Come back here!'

She spun away, laughing, and he raced after her.

Sparky and Clutch reached the mezzanine. Bright tongues of flame licked around the timbers. Suddenly a huge section of floor fell away, leaving just a pair of beams intact – twin tightropes across empty space. At the far end was the loading-bay window, directly above the front doors. It was the only way out. Sparky swallowed hard.

'Okay. We can do this,' he said to himself. 'I think . . .'

He edged out into space, high above the flames, his tyres feeling along the edge of the two beams.

'Don't look down, don't look down, don't look down.'

He looked down. A swirling firestorm boiled below, fiery tendrils reaching up at him. He squeezed his eyes shut.

After a moment he continued on, eyes still shut, judging the width of the two beams with the outer rims of his tyres. At last he reached the far end and gasped with relief.

'Okay, Clutch, now all we have to do is jump out this window . . .' He looked back over his shoulder. 'Clutch?'

Clutch was still back at the other end of the beams.

'Come on!' he called desperately, but Clutch shook his head. Sparky looked out the window to safety. He hesitated, then called back over his shoulder.

'Okay, hang on. I'm coming back.'

Gritting his teeth, he gingerly turned on the two beams, one wheel at a time – a delicate high-wire balancing trick. The flames were starting to lick around his fenders. One wheel slipped and for a terrible moment he teetered above the inferno. Then he regained his balance, steadied himself and headed back to Clutch.

'Listen to me, Clutch,' he said urgently. 'It's about to get really hot in here. Do you understand? You've got to believe in me. We can do this, together. Now, come on . . .'

He headed out again, backwards this time, keeping his eyes fixed on Clutch's face. Clutch edged out after him. The beams creaked and groaned. The flames roared higher and higher all around.

It didn't look like they were going to make it . . .

Prudence was in a terrible state when she saw Zoe and Hercules coming her way.

'Zoe! Quickly. The workshop is on fire!'

They hurried up to the burning building. Zoe tried dousing the flames with her water cannon, but the searing heat drove her back. The workshop was beyond saving.

A moment later, Digger and Bullworth raced up. Prudence turned to them with dull eyes.

'Sparky's in there . . .'

They looked on helplessly as the flames roared higher.

The sound of breaking glass came from overhead. The watching TruckDogs looked up. Amidst a shower of shattered glass, Sparky burst through the window high above them, surrounded by a halo of flames. Clutch followed, bringing the window frame and most of the wall with him.

Sparky sailed through the air and, for a moment, the scene seemed to go in slow motion. The Mongrel Pack watched open-mouthed as he floated silently earthward, wheels spinning, ears flapping.

Then sound and motion returned. Sparky thudded to the ground with a sickening crunch. His new suspension shattered, retaining bolts and air-hoses shooting off the ends of the hydraulic pistons with a hiss and whoosh. But apart from being bruised, winded and somewhat overheated, he was otherwise unharmed and very much alive.

He staggered a little, then regained his balance amidst the cheering of his friends. A moment later Clutch slammed down in a shower of falling debris and sat there, dazed, amongst the rubble.

Prudence eyed the monster uncertainly.

'And this would be . . . ?'

'His name's Clutch,' said Sparky, patting the monster on the cab.

Clutch gave him a big wet lick across the face. Sparky screwed up his nose and laughed.

'And I think he's my friend!'

Suddenly Zoe called out. 'Sparky, look. Your mum's in trouble.'

Up the road at the Town Hall, Mayor Plugg stood on the porch as a particularly unpleasant-looking RottWheeler slowly advanced up the ramp towards her, snarling.

'I am warning you, in my official capacity as Mayor, to stay where you are,' she was saying, 'or you will feel the full weight of the law.' She held up her big mayoral medallion on its blue sash. The RottWheeler glanced at the medallion, grinned and kept coming.

'Right, then.' Mrs Plugg whipped off the medallion with

her teeth, swung it round and caught him a terrific blow on the side of the cab. The RottWheeler stopped in surprise, smiled stupidly and rolled over, senseless.

'Heavy, isn't it?' said Mayor Plugg.

'Way to go, Mum!' Sparky called, then turned to his friends. 'My mum can look after herself. She's cool.'

They nodded in agreement.

But the other townsfolk were still in the thick of things. The RottWheelers had regrouped and were mounting a fresh attack from the hill behind the remains of the windmill.

The Mongrels headed off to help and Sparky made to follow. Suddenly Clutch growled. Sparky looked at him in alarm but then saw what the huge brute was looking at – Mr Big slipping away down the narrow lane at the side of the general store. His eyes narrowed.

'Okay, I see him. Stay close.'

Mr Big peeped round the far end of the general store, checking that the coast was clear. The open desert lay beyond.

'Leaving without your fuel? But we told you we had enough to see you on your way.'

Mr Big spun around to find Sparky and Clutch standing behind him. Clutch growled and bared his teeth. Quick as a flash, Mr Big dived through the gaping hole in the side of the store. Clutch sprang after him with a roar.

'No, boy! Heel!' yelled Sparky. Clutch stopped and looked back with a bewildered whine.

'We don't eat baddies round here. We catch them and chuck 'em in jail. Understand?'

Clutch nodded.

'Okay, then. Let's get him!'

Sparky squinted as he adjusted his eyes to the dim light inside the store. All around were dusty aisles loaded with produce. There was no sign of Mr Big. He motioned down one of the aisles.

'You take engine oils,' he whispered to Clutch. 'I'll take worming tablets and flea powder. Keep your engine low.'

Sparky crept down his aisle towards the back of the store.

Mr Big meanwhile had made his way down an aisle lined with canned dog food and packets of Doggy Bites. At the back of the shop there was a storeroom door. An exit sign glowed above it. Suddenly he heard the sound of an engine in the next aisle – and snuffling. It was Clutch. Mr Big froze, sweat trickling down his windscreen. His eyes fell on a bag of Doggy Bites.

Clutch was sniffing along the bottom of the shelving when a Doggy Bite rolled out in front of him and across the floor. He followed it, sniffed, and gobbled it up.

Another followed, and another.

In the next aisle Mr Big listened to Clutch chomping away. He poured the rest of the bag of Doggy Bites under the shelves, then crept across to the back door, his own engine noise covered by Clutch's gobbling.

Meanwhile Sparky reached the check-out counter at the front of the store. He looked back just as Mr Big disappeared into the back room.

He hurried down the aisle to find Clutch gorging himself. Clutch looked up, mouth full, then remembered what he should be doing and swallowed with an apologetic smile.

'He went that way.' Sparky motioned towards the door. 'You go round the side to the back lane and cut him off.'

Clutch glanced longingly at the remaining Doggy Bites strewn over the floor, then headed off. Sparky tried the door to the back room – but it had been barred from the inside.

The storeroom was dark, the only light coming from narrow cracks in the weatherboard wall. A rear door opened out into the laneway beyond. Mr Big made for it. But a strange sound made him stop. He peered into the gloom and could just make out a large iron gate. Strangely, there seemed to be a set of horns entangled in it. The gate rose into the air, revealing a most unexpected sight – a very large TruckRam with a thick layer of mush around its muzzle. It had been happily scoffing on a bag of feed when Mr Big burst in. Now it snorted loudly, covering Mr Big's surprised face in a thick layer of soggy oats.

Inside the general store, Sparky was still wondering how to get into the back room when the door suddenly exploded into a million pieces. He leapt back as Mr Big shot out, squealing in terror, followed closely by the TruckRam.

'YAAAAH!' yelled Sparky.

'AAAAAAAAH!' screamed Mr Big.

'BAAAAAAAAAAAA! roared the TruckRam.

Mr Big landed on the Doggy Bites and spun out of control down the aisle, straight through the check-out and out the front door. He tumbled down the steps and sprawled into the street. An instant later the TruckRam burst through the front of the store, leaving a gaping hole where the door had been.

Before Mr Big could collect himself, the TruckRam bent its head, picked him up with the gate and sent him flying clear across the road. He crashed through the roof of Scratchly's Fencing Supplies. Bales of barbed wire flew up into the air. A mighty yelp of pain came from within.

The TruckRam snorted, looked around and galloped off as Sparky skidded out of the ruined store. Clutch joined him, panting. Sparky looked around urgently but Mr Big was nowhere in sight.

There was a crash and a curse from across the way and Mr Big backed painfully out into the road in a tangle of barbed wire.

'Need any help?' called Sparky.

Mr Big looked up. Clutch snarled and leapt forward. Mr Big squealed and bolted, hoops of wire trailing from his bumpers.

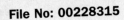

TRUCKDOGS

File No: 00228315

NAME: HUBCAP TOWNSFOLK

NAME: MRS DOGSBODY (Spaniel/Scissor-lift)

NAME: MR DOGSBODY (Basset Hound/Mobile Crane)

NAME: MR BARKER (Corgi/Delivery Van)

NAME: IDA FLEASOME (Beagle/Fiat 500)

NAME: EDNA FLEASOME (Basengi/Trabant 601)

They whipped about, lashing at his rear end. Sparky and Clutch raced after him.

'Yeow! Yipe! Ow!'

Sparky and Clutch leapt after him.

After they had gone, there was a groan of splintered timbers and the whole general store teetered and collapsed in a cloud of flea powder, worming tablets and Doggy Bites.

While the Battle of Hubcap raged, Throttle had been hiding, watching. Now, as it became clear she realised the RottWheelers were being thrashed, she snuck away from behind the fuel shed, slipping across the rubble and coarse grass behind the outbuildings and onto the road out of town.

She looked back. A plume of smoke rose into the air.

'Stinking town. Fuel was low-grade rubbish anyway.'

She turned back to the road and gasped in shock. There in front of her, blocking the road, was Rex. His head was bowed. She stopped dead in her tracks.

'What are you doing here?'

Rex's missing wheel had been replaced with a traction-engine flywheel, and his funnel with a set of old V8 extractor pipes – pretty hot-looking, in fact. He looked up slowly and fixed her with a steady gaze.

'I've come to get my spanner back.'

Up in town, the last RottWheeler sagged, defeated, to the ground. The Mongrels and the townsfolk looked around, only now able to stop and take in the smouldering workshop and the pile of rubble that had been the general store.

Hercules whistled through his grille. 'Made a bit of a mess, eh?'

'Yep,' nodded Digger. 'It's what we're good at.'

'It certainly is,' came a voice.

They turned to find Mayor Plugg standing by them. They gulped, but she winked. 'Don't worry about it, fellas. Never liked that general store anyway.' She smiled at their stunned expressions. 'By the way, it's good to see you back.'

Just then Prudence called out from up by the garage. She was looking down the road. 'It's Rex!'

Mayor Plugg, Hercules, Digger, Prudence, Zoe and the towns-folk all gathered at the edge of the forecourt to watch. Down on the Great Outback Highway, Rex and Throttle eyed each other – the powerful young dragster and the worn-out old tractor.

'So what are you now?' Throttle scoffed. 'Some kind of road warrior?'

Rex said nothing.

Throttle laughed. 'And you think you can just take your spanner back, is that it?'

Rex nodded. 'Yup.'

Throttle's eyes narrowed. She sized him up – the bald tyres, the weedy frame, the rusty bolts. He was no match for her.

'You old fool.' She held the spanner up in front of him. 'So come and get it.'

Rex rolled forward. Throttle leapt at him, intending to take him out in one swift move. Rex moved deftly aside and she crunched to the ground, surprised and winded.

'One–nil,' said Hercules, up at the petrol station.

Throttle picked herself up and lashed out with her rear wheels. Rex grabbed her by the axle and flipped her upside down. She crashed down on her cab.

'Two–nil,' said Zoe.

Throttle was up again in an instant. She and Rex circled one another, alert, watching.

'You belong in a junkyard,' she spat. 'You're just a clapped-out tractor, old and weak and foolish.'

'While you are young and strong and arrogant,' said Rex. 'An interesting contest, no?'

Digger leant across to Prudence and whispered, 'He's going all oriental again.'

Prudence whispered back, 'I think he has a Japanese drive-train.'

Down on the highway, Throttle taunted Rex. 'So come on, old tractor. Bring it on. Show me what you've got.'

'Patience is a TruckDog's greatest ally.'

'Patience? I'm a girl who likes a bit of action!'

On the word 'action' she lunged again, but Rex sent her sprawling behind him in the dirt. He didn't even look around.

Bullworth nodded appreciatively. 'Double points. Four–nil.'

Throttle turned with a snarl and leapt at Rex's unguarded back. The onlookers on the forecourt cringed at the coming impact, but at the last moment Rex half turned and raised his front wheel. Throttle slammed into it like a TruckBug hitting a windscreen on the freeway. She reeled away, stunned, tottered for a moment, then slumped to the ground.

Rex rolled up to her and picked up his spanner. His eyes flickered as he noted the damage.

'You're lucky I didn't know about this before. I might have got mad.'

Throttle opened a bleary eye and groaned.

'Five, six, seven, eight, nine and ten,' said Hercules. 'No contest. Game to Rex.'

'Yay, Rex!' shouted Zoe. 'Way to go!'

'Woo hoo!' hooted Digger.

Suddenly Mr Dogsbody called out in warning. Embers from the smouldering workshop had lodged in the grass by the fuel shed. Brake, still trapped under the overloaded tanker, saw the flames begin to take hold and yelled out.

'Help . . . help me!'

Hercules, Digger and Prudence were closest. They rushed over and tried to push the stranded tanker out of danger. Mayor Plugg joined them but Brake was stuck fast under the weight of the tanker.

'Zoe! Quick!' yelled Hercules but Zoe gestured helplessly. 'I'm out of water!'

Then Bullworth rolled up to the tanker. Harnessing an inner strength, he lowered his mighty head and began to push. The tanker slid slowly but surely away from the shed. Two metres, five metres, ten metres. Everyone watched, spellbound. Fifteen metres, twenty metres . . .

Finally Prudence called out. 'Okay, Bullworth, okay! That's enough. Any more and he'll die of friction burns.'

The flames licked around the fuel-shed door. The TruckDogs backed away, bracing themselves for the blast. At that moment, the TruckRam trotted around the back of the garage – a bizarre sight, its gate held high above its head. It looked at the flames in alarm and jumped clear of them – onto the roof of the shed . . .

KAAAAAAAA-BOOOM!

The shed rocketed straight up in the air, taking the TruckRam with it, and vanished out of sight in the clouds of smoke.

Prudence turned to Digger, not quite able to accept what she had seen. 'Did you . . . was that . . . ?'

Digger was equally stunned. 'Yeah. I think so.'

At the other end of town, Sparky and Clutch raced after Mr Big, hot on his tail. The barbed wire hanging off Mr Big's bumper came loose and wrapped itself around

Clutch. He stopped to disentangle himself. Sparky sped on.

Mr Big scurried around the remains of the workshop and into the petrol-station forecourt – and found the entire town waiting for him. He screeched to a stop. A moment later, Sparky came hurtling round the corner and skidded to a halt by the tanker. Mr Big looked around desperately. A wall of grim-faced TruckDogs looked back at him. He turned and saw Sparky by himself, without Clutch.

With the desperation of a cornered animal he flung himself at Sparky, pointy little teeth bared in a look of pure hatred. Sparky recoiled, caught unawares by the speed and savageness of the attack. Rex, who had chugged up to the forecourt, yelled out to him and sent the silver spanner spinning through the air. Sunlight flashed off it as it flew towards the tanker.

In an instant Sparky saw where it was heading. He jumped – five metres clear, no hydraulic assistance – and caught the spanner between his teeth. Twisting in midair, he locked the spanner onto the pressure-release valve on the back of the tanker and turned it. Fuel blasted out of the valve, a sudden powerful jet. It hit Mr Big right in the face, shooting straight up his nose.

Mr Big was flung backwards along the ground. He gasped, inhaling several litres of fuel, flooding his engine. There was a high-pitched screeching sound followed by a muffled *pthoonk!* as his motor seized and exploded. Smoke billowed from under his bonnet. A second, larger explosion detonated the fuel tank. His doors flew off and the gearbox dropped out onto the ground, spilling cogs and sump oil all over the road.

He lay there, a broken wreck, at Sparky's wheels, and groaned. A small black dot appeared in the centre of his roof, growing rapidly larger. Sparky looked up and backed away. A moment later, the TruckRam – minus gate and looking extremely surprised – landed full on the little tyrant, squashing him flat.

'Baaaaaaaa!'

A second later the gate clanged down in front of Mr Big's face, the vertical iron bars looking for all the world like the bars of a prison cell.

Sparky closed the fuel valve and regarded Mr Big sternly.

'Bad dog.'

Mayor Plugg came up to her son, shaking her head in wonder. 'Where did you learn to do that? More bad influences, I assume?'

Sparky grinned.

Rex rolled up to join them. Mayor Plugg looked at him. The tractor shrugged. 'Young fella has a natural talent.'

'Thanks, Rex,' said Sparky, giving back the spanner. 'I owe you, big time.'

Mrs Plugg regarded Rex with new appreciation. 'You know, a pup needs a . . . well . . . a role model. Thank you, Rex.'

He acknowledged her with a polite nod.

Just then Clutch arrived, chomping on the remains of the barbed wire. A murmur ran through the crowd and they backed away nervously.

'It's okay,' said Sparky. 'He's with me.'

Clutch gave him another big lick across the face. The townsfolk looked on, gob-smacked. Then everyone began to talk at
once. Clutch saw his former master behind bars and howled
in approval.

'Hooray for Sparky!' called out Prudence.

The crowd barked and beeped.

'Three cheers for the Mongrel Pack!' shouted Mrs Plugg.
The crowd honked and howled.

'Let's hear it for Hubcap!' yelled Hercules.

And the crowd went totally wild.

TRUCK**DOGS**

8316

NAME: DESERTDOG (LEADER)

BREED/MAKE: Dingo/4 x 4
COLOUR: Yellow
IDENTIFYING MARKS: Short one eye
TEMPERAMENT: Savage

FILE INFO:
Leader of the DesertDogs that inhabit outback areas north and north-east of Combustion City. Potentially v. dangerous. Doesn't like loud noises.

SPECIFICATIONS:
Engine: Generally V6 (3.2 – 4.3 l)
Fuel Requirements: Whatever the tribe catches
Maintenance: Not likely!

(Note also: Marsupial/Bicycle TruckRoo)

BITE FOUR

few days later, the iron bars of the gate had been replaced by the real thing. Mr Big, worse for wear and nastier than ever, took up residence in the Hubcap Jailhouse at the back of the Town Hall. Throttle had the cell next door. Sparky could see them looking out of their barred windows as he crossed the street, past the garage where the new workshop was already under construction, on his way to Memorial Park.

The two inmates couldn't see each other but that didn't stop them having a lively conversation.

'Take all the fuel,' sneered Throttle. 'Every last drop. Nice call, Boss.'

'Ah shut up, you whingeing mutt,' snapped Mr Big.

'Don't you tell me to shut up, you overgrown TruckRat. I could've told you all that fuel was too heavy.'

'Oh, so now you're the big genius? Left your run a bit late, haven't you, you flea-bitten tramp?'

'I've *always* been smarter than you. Everyone knew that, except you. They respected me!'

'By everyone I assume you mean that mangy bunch of ungrateful mutts who have run off and left us both to rot? Respect, hah!'

Sparky shook his head and continued on into the park where a big celebration was getting underway. A huge marquee had been set up amongst the trees, giving the park a great party atmosphere. In the middle of the tent stood the statue of Lord Hubcap, back on its pedestal, still missing an ear but otherwise intact.

Mr Dogsbody was hanging fairy lights high up in the branches with his crane. Farmer Howell was directing operations. He called out to Mr Scratchly. 'Okay, switch them on.'

'What's that?'

'We've finished. You can switch them on now.'

'Eh?'

'I said . . .' began Farmer Howell, but Mr Scratchly laughed and flipped the switch.

'I hear ya, Windy. I hear ya.'

The lights blinked to life, twinkling amongst the gum leaves.

'Ooooh. Aren't they pretty?' cried Ida.

Edna looked at the lights, tut-tutting in disapproval. 'Waste of energy. What is this town coming to?'

'Well, they look pretty to me,' said Ida.

Edna looked at her sharply. 'Ida! You're not thinking for yourself, are you?'

'Oh no, Edna,' she said. 'I would *never* do that.'

Edna looked away, satisfied. Ida glanced at her, then looked back at the lights, smiling.

Back up on the main street, Brake rolled by, a broom and shovel in his mouth. He was hauling a wagon with a sign reading 'Hubcap Pooper Patrol'. Mrs Dogsbody followed close behind.

'There's another one,' she said, pointing at the ground.

Brake scooped up the offending article, plopped it in the wagon and rolled on.

'We'll make a good citizen of you yet,' she said. 'Look, there's another one.'

Brake just grunted.

After they passed by, Clutch came cavorting across the street with a rusty old wrench in his mouth. He raced up to Sparky, dropped the wrench and sat expectantly, stumpy tail thumping the ground. Sparky threw it across the park, high into the air. Clutch bounded after it.

'This time with a double pike and turn!' Sparky called after him. Clutch leapt, somersaulted and landed with the wrench in his mouth.

'Good boy, Clutch! Off you go.'

Clutch gambolled off happily. Rex rolled up next to Sparky and watched him go. 'He's almost as good as you.

Might make a fine member of the Mongrel Pack one day.'

Sparky smiled up at Rex. Then he noticed that the old tractor had his tool kit with him.

'You're leaving.'

Rex nodded. 'Yup.'

'But there's so much work to do. A town needs a mechanic. You know that.'

'It surely does. That's why I want you to have this.' He gave Sparky his big silver spanner. 'It's got a couple of dents, I'm afraid, but otherwise it's in good working order.'

Sparky took the spanner wonderingly. He looked back at Rex with shining eyes. Just then, Mayor Plugg rolled up.

'So, Rex,' she said. 'I can't persuade you to stay?'

Rex shook his head. 'No, ma'am.'

'Well, I thank you for all you've done for us. This town is the richer for your being here.'

Rex thanked Mayor Plugg and turned to Sparky.

'You take care, young fella.'

Sparky nodded and bit his lip.

'Where are you going?' he asked suddenly.

Rex thought about it for a moment, then smiled. 'Somewhere I haven't been before, I reckon. Guess I'll know when I get there.'

He chugged off.

Mother and son watched him go. Mayor Plugg sighed quietly.

'A pup needs a father.'

Sparky grinned at her. 'Not with a mum like you around.'

She looked down at him and smiled. 'Come on, you – there's official business to take care of.'

Sparky spun the spanner and flipped it into his tray.

Mayor Plugg was taken aback. 'Where did you . . . ?' She stopped and laughed. 'Never mind.'

They returned to the celebrations together. Sparky went to stand with the other Mongrels to one side of the official dais. The gang were without their armour now and looking unusually clean – polished paintwork, clean tyres – no dirt under the mudflaps today. Mayor Plugg addressed the townsfolk.

'Citizens of Hubcap, your attention, please. It is with great pleasure that I hereby award these six most excellent young TruckDogs the Hubcap Medal of Honour, and present them with the official Car Keys to the City.'

Six cute little TruckPups trotted up, each with a medal, a key and a bunch of flowers in its mouth. Sparky's TruckPup was the one who had tried to pee on the head of Lord Hubcap. Sparky winked at him. The TruckPup wagged his tail at high speed – he was a tiny version of Sparky.

The Mongrel Pack – Hercules, Bullworth, Prudence, Digger, Zoe and Sparky – turned to face the crowd. The entire town erupted in a fanfare of cheering and beeping. Sparky and his friends beamed with pleasure. Every TruckDog has its day.

'Please accept these as tokens of our thanks for your gallantry in saving our town,' continued Mayor Plugg. 'You are truly cherished members of this community. Welcome home!'

'Home,' said Zoe. Her eyes were shining.

'It's got a nice ring to it,' nodded Digger.

'I think I'm going to cry,' sniffed Bullworth.

Prudence passed him an oil rag. 'Take it easy, big boy.' He blew his nose nosily.

And she blinked back a tear herself.

Hercules moved forward and cleared his throat. The townsfolk fell silent.

'Well,' he said. 'Speaking for the Pack, it's no secret that we've never had a lot of time for you folks. And you've had no time for us. You're old – but that's not your fault, any more than it's our fault for being young.' He paused. 'So I guess if you can learn to cope with us, then we can learn to cope with you.' He shrugged. 'What say we start from there and see how we go?'

'Sounds good to me,' smiled Mayor Plugg, and the crowd cheered in approval. 'Furthermore, I hereby declare that from this day forth all TruckDogs shall have the right to rev their engines as they please . . .'

'. . . play street football . . .' said Mr Dogsbody.

'. . . listen to raucous music . . .' added Mr Scratchly.

'. . . go drag racing . . .' called out Ida.

'Drag racing?' said a shocked Edna.

'. . . leap the occasional sheep . . .' said Farmer Howell.

'. . . and generally act like kids – loud, fast and covered in mud!' concluded Mayor Plugg. 'And that includes us vintage TruckDogs as well.'

The crowd erupted again, tossing their hubcaps into the air in celebration.

Out on the highway Rex paused and smiled as the cheering and beeping wafted across the desert on the cool evening air. He sighed, looking back at the twinkling lights, and thought for a moment. Then he turned and chugged off up the road.

Back up on the hill, Sparky emerged from the marquee and looked out across the desert. He saw a figure in the distance, a lone TruckDog on an endless highway. But as he watched, the figure softly vanished, leaving the road empty. Sparky blinked. The road shifted and shimmered in his eyes. He wiped away a tear.

Then, with a deep breath, he turned and drove back towards the lights.

A moment later, the soft dusky-pink blanket of twilight closed in gently on the desert and the Great Outback Highway too faded away into the night.

THE END

LAST NIP

Far out in the desert, a lone TruckDog flees squealing from a pack of howling DesertDogs. He looks familiar – a corgi/delivery van with a squint.

He swerves desperately this way and that, DesertDogs snapping at his heels, until the leader of the pack, a big one-eyed brute, brings him down with a crunch. The rest of the pack gather round and sniff curiously.

Suddenly he pops up again, catching the DesertDogs by surprise, and races away, zigzagging madly towards the horizon. The DesertDogs howl and set off after him, disappearing in a cloud of dust.

At least he has a full tank of fuel.

'Howowowowoooo!'

A note regarding

TRUCKBUGS

The world of TruckDogs is home to a number of other species which have evolved along similar lines to the dominant canine/vehicular life forms. They include TruckSheep, TruckRodents and TruckChickens. The most diverse group, however, is the TruckBugs. Below are some of the more common TruckBugs that can be found in the 16 Illustrated Plates.

1 LADYBIRD/ROADSTER   *Coccinellidae automotum*

2 STAG BEETLE/FORKLIFT   *Lucanidae lifterupus*

3 WEEVIL/ROAD SWEEPER   *Chrysolopus cleaneria*

4 ANT/CEMENT MIXER   *Myrmecia minimixia*

5 BUTTERFLY/HANG GLIDER (PLUS ANT)   *Nymphalidae wheeee!*

6 DRAGONFLY/HELICOPTER/EXCAVATOR   *Aeshna whirli diggeri*

7 SNAIL/HOTROD   *Helix turbochargeum*

8 DUNG BEETLE/BULLDOZER   *Scarabaeidae gruntae*

9 MOSQUITO/AUGER   *Culicidae drillium*

10 SCORPION/SCISSOR-LIFT   *Centruroides scissori*

11 MAGGOT/BUS   *Musca commuterae*

12 WASP/JET FIGHTER   *Hemithynnus veryfastilis*

13 MANTID/ROAD GRADER   *Archimantis flattenouttera*

14 RED-BACK SPIDER/HOVERCRAFT   *Latrodectus amphibiosae*

15 GRASSHOPPER/MOTORBIKE   *Monistria brrmbrrm*

16 MOTH/AEROPLANE   *Oxycanus extrabitattheendus*